UNFORGETTABLE

Indulgence series

A NOVELLA

By
New York Times, Wall Street Journal, and USA Today
bestselling author
Aleatha Romig

COPYRIGHT AND LICENSE INFORMATION

This book is available in ebook from most online retailers

2019 Edition License

DISCLAIMER

The INDULGENCE series contains novellas designed to bring out the harbored fantasies often buried deep inside. If you're ready to give that a try, enjoy this fun, sexy journey into the world of exploration and find your happily ever after.

BLURB

UNFORGETTABLE
Indulgence series
A NOVELLA

MARJI

Working for a therapist who specializes in exploring hidden desires sounds like a dream job. It is if hearing other people's fantasies and discoveries is your cup of tea. The problem is that I'm tired of hearing about them. I want more. I want to experience them.

What harm will it do if I indulge just one time?
That's where *Lace and Leather* comes in.
A falsified referral and I'm in the door.
One visit is all I want.

LUCAS

Sometimes plans change. Sometimes life throws curves. Sometimes we must force ourselves to move forward and take life a day at a time.

I did all that.
Now I want more.

I want to remember what it is like to do more than exist, what it's like to live. I want to learn if the desires I once possessed still exist. I'm not looking for anyone to replace my wife or the mother of my daughter. I only want to see if I'm still the man I was.

That's why I decide to return to a place where that discovery is possible, *Lace and Leather*.
One visit is all I want.

From New York Times, Wall Street Journal, and USA Today bestselling author Aleatha Romig comes another of her steamy novellas exploring hidden desires. UNFORGETTABLE is a stand-alone story in the INDULGENCE series.

*Warning: reading may set your e-reader on fire while bringing a smile to your face.

Have you been Aleatha'd?

MARJI

"The client blushed as she recalled the setting, describing the scene as she entered the cabin. With each implement she recalled, her cheeks grew redder until she finally apologized. I questioned as to whether talking about their encounter made her anxious or embarrassed. With a sly grin toward her husband, the client replied, 'It makes me want to go back.'"

Pulling the earbuds from my ears, I shake my head, pushing the visuals from my mind. With a quick save, using the clients' identification number instead of name, I close out their records and complete the transcription of Dr. Kizer's appointment notes from the day before.

Looking down at the corner of my computer screen, I see that it is nearly seven at night, almost time to leave work and live. That's what is supposed to happen at this time of night. I know that it is because I've read about it in the novels on my Kindle. I've seen the images on television or in movies. I even transcribe a therapist's detailed notes telling me that is the way it should be.

They're all the same.

They're evidence that not everyone lives for work, novels, and Netflix.

The images and stories are of people shedding their work or career responsibilities, and like a butterfly, freeing themselves from their daytime cocoon, the drab outer layer exfoliating and the bright, colorful wings stretching until the butterfly is free and able to take flight.

"Thank you, Dr. Kizer," Mr. Williams says as his wife smiles, her cheeks blushed from whatever discussion has been happening behind Dr. Kizer's closed office door.

The discussion I will be turning into records tomorrow.

That knowledge causes me to straighten my shoulders, not wanting to give away my connection to the clients' intimated details.

As the couple comes to a stop in front of my desk, I can't help but notice the admiration and adoration they share. It radiates off of each of them. There's no hidden anxiety or concern. It's pure, unadulterated trust and esteem, as if they're the only two people in the room. Forget that. They're the only two people now in the world.

Mrs. Williams's head shakes as she tilts her forehead against her husband's shoulder with a soft giggle.

"Um," I say, clearing my throat. "Would you like to schedule your appointment for next week?"

Mr. Williams looks my direction. "Make that two weeks. We're following Dr. Kizer's advice and taking a week away..." He looks down lovingly at his wife. "...just the two of us."

Mrs. Williams nods. "I sent my mom a text and she's going to stay with the kids. I didn't think I was ready for an entire week, but I am."

Please no details.

That's my thought as her cheeks again fill with crimson.

"Then, two weeks," I say, pulling up Dr. Kizer's schedule on my screen. "Two weeks on Thursday at six p.m.?"

"That's perfect," Mr. Williams says as he enters the appointment into his phone. "Oh Marji, do we talk to you about the use of Dr. Kizer's cabin?"

"For next week?" I ask a bit wearily.

"Yes."

I sit taller. "I'm sorry. The cabins are all booked in advance." I hit a few keys on the keyboard, suddenly feeling the same disappointment that is now emanating from the two people before me.

"Dr. Kizer said there was a recent cancellation," Mr. Williams says. "Can you please check?"

"Next week is our anniversary," Mrs. Williams adds with a hopeful grin. "Seven years and it is better than ever." She sighs. "Better than I could have hoped for."

"If this doesn't work out..." Mr. Williams's words to

his wife disappear as I type upon the keyboard until the cabin rental schedule appears before me.

To my surprise, there is an opening. "Well, Dr. Kizer was right."

"She always is," Mrs. Williams says, her smile returning bigger than ever as she still holds tightly to her husband's arm.

I don't want to think about what will be happening at the cabin—the scene and the implements: crops, gags, and restraints to name a few. It's really none of my business what two consenting adults choose to do in their spare time. I mean, it's their decision.

I could pretend to be naïve, tell myself that they're going to rent the cabin for a week to hike the trails or picnic near the lake. I could tell myself that it's no different than any other rental, a Vrbo or a time-share.

If I did tell myself any of the above stories, I wouldn't believe me.

Along with scheduling Dr. Kizer's clients, seeing them come in on the verge of marital or relationship collapse and observing their transformations, singularly as well as a couple, as I was doing a few minutes ago, I also transcribe her notes. With an earbud in my ear, I listen to the details as my fingers type, creating a printable record of words of thoughts and feelings that should only be discussed in private.

Of course, what I do is confidential. I wouldn't share a word.

I'm bound to the ethics of my job. That doesn't mean

I don't retain the information, sometimes think about it, and sometimes imagine what it would be like to be one of these wives.

Please don't assume I am out to wreck a marriage. That's the farthest thing from the truth. I don't want any of the husbands that come in here for counseling.

No, I want my own.

I'm not even looking for a *husband*, just a man who is capable of indulging in a few fantasies I can't seem to unimagine.

I write the six-digit code on a card and hand it to Mr. Williams. "Here's the code to unlock the cabin. The address is on the back. It's very isolated. There are directions online at the website on the card. Many GPS receivers have difficulty finding it. Please notify the number on the front of the card if you have any specific requests prior to your arrival. Your rental begins on Saturday. Be sure to notify the rental company of those requests by Friday."

"Specific requests?" Mrs. Williams asks. "I was under the impression it's fully...um...furnished...stocked..."

"Yes," I say, working to keep a neutral smile plastered on my lips. "The cabin is furnished with everything Dr. Kizer has mentioned or you mentioned and more. It's the food and drink that you can either bring or it can be stocked." I take a deep breath. "Perhaps you have diet restrictions? And if you want anything particular that hasn't been mentioned, the number on the front can help."

"Do they...?" Mrs. Williams swallows. "...know our names?"

I shake my head. "No, ma'am. This is part of Dr. Kizer's therapy. It's completely confidential. I also wrote your ID number on the back. That is how they know you."

She nodded as she looked up at her husband with her eyes wide. "We should talk...about things. I read about something once..."

Mr. Williams stands taller. His action silences her words, yet by the gleam in his gaze, it's obvious that he's more than interested to hear her thoughts. Turning back to me, he nods. "Thank you, Marji. We'll see you and Dr. Kizer in two weeks."

"Bye." *Have a great time.* I don't say the last part, trying to squelch any images of their future before they take root in my mind.

As the door to the front office closes and the Williamses disappear, I lean back in my chair and exhale. I've been working here for over two years. You'd think those conversations would get easier.

"Marji?"

I turn as Dr. Ami Kizer steps from her office. In a gray pencil skirt, white silk blouse, and closed-toe high-heel pumps, no one would know that this proper lady spends her days discussing and encouraging sexual exploration.

"Yes?"

"Can you please close up? I have to leave early."

"Sure thing. Do you need today's notes transcribed tonight?"

"No," she says with a wave of her hand. "I have them all recorded. They can wait until tomorrow. You deserve to enjoy your night like everyone else."

Like everyone else.

"Okay."

"Is everything all right, Marji?"

I force a smile. "I'm your office manager, remember? I'm not a client."

"No, but you're also a friend. I couldn't keep this place running without you. If you ever want to talk..."

"I'm not exactly eligible for couples counseling." I make a scrunched face. "I'm minus the part about a couple."

Dr. Kizer shrugged. "The world is filled with halves of couples waiting to find one another. It's a matter of looking in the right place."

"And where would that be?" I ask.

"Sometimes where you least expect it. Have a good night, Marji."

"You too, Dr. Kizer. See you tomorrow."

LUCAS

"*D*addy," Callie calls as she tugs my hand toward the refrigerated section of the grocery store, pointing up at the cups of pudding. "I like chocolate. You said I could have chocolate pudding for dinner."

My head shakes. "Callie girl, I said you could have chocolate pudding for dessert. Dinner isn't pudding."

"But I like pudding the bestest."

I suppose when I imagined parenthood, I saw myself more as my father had been, present yet not omnipresent. I had delusions of coming home from work to a clean home with dinner cooking in the oven and my wife greeting me with a cold beer or maybe a tumbler with two fingers of bourbon.

Okay.

I admit my illusions weren't quite that misogynistic. I can't help that I watched reruns of *Happy Days* or even *Leave it to Beaver* as a kid. My dad wasn't that

1950's, nor was my mom. My dad was hands-on and a good guy. He still is. He and my mom are not only great examples of parents but they're also fantastic grandparents to Callie.

The difference with illusions and reality is that now I'm all Callie has in the parent department. I'm Dad and Mom. I'm the fun one and the tough one. It would be great to let my daughter eat chocolate pudding for dinner, watch cartoons, and fall asleep on the living room couch. No, a fun dad would make it even better. Together we could fall asleep under a tent made from sheets in the middle of the living room.

I wanted that, but life decided to throw us a curveball.

Callie's mom is no longer with us, and I miss her every day.

I've tried it all to move on. I've tried grief counseling, single-parent classes, and getting involved in Callie's preschool. The latter was a disaster.

Do you know how many dads attend parent meetings alone?

Do you know how many moms feel it is their calling in life to keep that dad involved?

The answer to that would be too many, especially too many with wedding rings present on their left hand.

The truth is that I'm not looking for a wife to greet me at the door. I'm not looking to share parenting responsibilities of my precious daughter. I would simply like to feel that I'm more than a daddy once in a while.

I'd like to remember what it was like to be a man in control.

Take my word for it, there is absolutely no control with a four-, almost five-year-old. The 1950s TV shows may give that misconception, but my precious little girl knows what she wants. I love that quality and want to encourage her. However, sometimes it would be nice if I too could get what I want, a grown woman with similar—complementing—desires.

The memories of Beth and having that type of relationship are fading, and I'm not certain I will ever get them back.

I corral Callie after throwing two four-packs of pudding in our cart and head toward the produce aisle.

While I'm not looking for anyone or even someone, there are times when a woman catches my eye. At this moment, it's the blonde inspecting fresh lettuce that I notice. She seems vaguely familiar, yet I can't seem to place her, when all of a sudden, Callie bolts from my side to the strawberries, plowing face-first into the blonde's side.

"Oh," she says as she reaches out and secures Callie, stopping her from tumbling to the floor.

"I'm sorry," Callie says shyly as she stares up at the woman.

"Are you all right?" the woman asks, surveying my rambunctious daughter.

"Yes," Callie says, "I was looking at the strawsberries."

"Strawberries," I correct. "And not looking where she

was going." I give the lady a sheepish smile. "I apologize for the collision. It seems that these days we have two speeds, full throttle and sleep."

The blonde woman smiles and I try not to gasp. There's something about her that sparks life into my dead soul.

"No harm, no foul," she says. "I'm certainly not going to stand in the way of a child and healthy fruit." Her light-blue gaze leaves me and inspects my cart, taking an inventory of the pudding at the bottom of it.

"Well, it will be good to add something healthy," I say with a grin.

The blonde's head tilts. "I'm sorry, do we know one another?" She shakes her head. "I promise that wasn't a line. You just seem...familiar."

"I was thinking the same thing," I say honestly.

She extends her petite hand. "Hi, I'm Marji. Your daughter is delightful."

I take her hand. "I'm Luke and I have to agree...most of the time." In my mind I'm doing a strategical breakdown of women, especially pretty blondes who I might know. I'm mostly certain she's not one of the women from the preschool. As an architect I meet my fair share of women, but yet that doesn't feel right. There's no ring on her left hand, which would rule out couples who contract home designs from me, and I've only worked with a few single women. Of course, my mind goes to my late wife. "I'm sorry, perhaps you knew my wife, Beth McAroy?"

Her blue eyes grow wide. "Yes."

Just as quickly, I watch as the shadow of remorse surfaces. It is an emotion I am good at detecting.

"Oh, I was sorry to hear about the accident." She looks at Callie who is still lifting and inspecting plastic containers filled with strawberries and her volume lowers. "You're doing a great job with her." She shrugs. "I had just started working for Dr. Ami Kizer when...well, I'm sorry."

Dr. Kizer.

I hadn't thought about Dr. Kizer in years. She'd been the one who helped Beth and me get back on track. She'd been the one who encouraged us to be honest and explore our desires as well as our boundaries. I could look back on our time with Dr. Kizer with sadness for what I've lost, but instead, I choose to view it as one of the factors that made our marriage a success.

"I guess couples counseling doesn't work when you're alone," I say as Callie returns with two containers in hand, and I shake my head. "One."

"But, Daddy, this one has the hugest ones. We can dip them in the pudding. This one..." Her big green eyes stare upward as she lifts the other container. "...has baby ones and needs the daddy ones in the other one. I couldn't take one and not the other."

Marji grins. "I don't think you can argue with that logic."

With a sigh, I take the strawberry containers from

Callie and add them to our cart "It was nice to see you again, Marji."

"Um, Luke, it's up to you, but just so you know, once you're one of Dr. Kizer's clients, she is always willing to see you again. You know...even to talk."

I nod. "I'll give that some thought."

With a smile that reaches to her blue eyes, she grins at both me and Callie before she turns and walks away.

"Who was that lady?" Callie asks. "She was nice."

"She was."

"And pretty. She looks like Elsa."

Her comparison of Marji to one of her favorite cartoon characters makes me smile. "I guess she does. Now, let's find our dinner and go home."

"We have strawsberries?"

"Yes, and we'll eat them *after* dinner."

MARJI

I stare up at the sign through my windshield. It isn't like it is a flashing neon light advertising a tawdry sex club. The sign is classy and unobtrusive, a simple notice at the end of a driveway beside the large iron gate. To anyone driving by, it might be thought a private restaurant or a country club. In a way it's both. Back in the day it might have been called a gentlemen's club.

I know about *Lace and Leather* from my work.

It is an establishment often mentioned in Dr. Kizer's notes as a place for couples to investigate their desires. The private club offers all levels of BDSM involvement from voyeurism to active participation. It's also very exclusive. Clients come only through referrals from VIP members and everyone undergoes background checks including medical and psychological records.

While I'm not certain what brought me here tonight, I know it's what I've been thinking about for weeks, months, or maybe even years. Let's be honest, I've been thinking about it since I began working for Dr. Kizer. It was after the Williamses returned from their weeklong getaway that I couldn't shake the thoughts. Their contentment was contagious. It seems a stay in one of Dr. Kizer's cabins is literally just what the doctor ordered.

The cabin isn't an option for me.

Lace and Leather is.

As I transcribed the notes from the Williamses' session after their getaway, it was as if I had been there, a fly on the wall, so to speak. The cabin wasn't their first experience with BDSM. Yet it didn't seem as if they were experts, both venturing into this new world together, willingly accepting of and open to its wonders.

The notes describe both of their emotions and feelings. Dr. Kizer is one of the best at getting her clients to express their inner thoughts. She creates a safe environment where they both can share.

The notes from Mrs. Williams are the ones I couldn't forget. The way she described the week was erotic and enticing, as well as intriguing. Another component Dr. Kizer emphasizes is trust. Both parties must trust one another to be open and remain nonjudgmental. She stresses that there are no wrongs or rights in exploration, only missed opportunities.

Trust.

Try.

Be honest about what happens.

Try again or try something else.

From the notes, it seems as though their week was successful on many fronts.

Exploring this world with someone you trust would make entering it together possible. For someone like me who is new and without a trusted partner, I believe *Lace and Leather* may be my answer. According to Dr. Kizer's notes, the club has clients who will help people like me explore. People who are trusted.

I know that isn't the same thing as my trusting them, but it's a start.

While Dr. Kizer mostly sends couples, according to my research, *Lace and Leather* also accepts willing singles.

That's me.

A single.

I am not sure what I want to get out of this night or even if I can go through with it. I guess I'm tired of transcribing other people's unforgettable experiences and am ready to have one of my own.

Taking a deep breath, I pull my car back onto the dark, secluded street and turn into the entrance of the long driveway. After I enter a code into the small box near the entrance, the gate before me opens.

I may have facilitated my own invitation. I may have made the email sound like Dr. Kizer was referring one of her clients, including all of the background information as if she were. It was either that or admit to my boss what I wanted to do.

The way I look at it is that my facilitating the referral is kind of the same thing, without the middle man.

Well, that's what I keep telling myself.

My heart thumps faster as the gate slides to the side. Taking a deep breath, my grip on the steering wheel tightens. I press the accelerator and drive forward. The lights of the impressive large building come into view. It's a historic mansion that has been present in this rural area of Wisconsin for over a hundred years. Only in the last fifteen years has it been transformed into a private club.

According to lore, the home was built by a wealthy family who came to this area from Canada. I doubt that when they had this masterpiece of a home constructed they had any idea what it would become. It's not that it is now a blatant, crude sex club. On the contrary, *Lace and Leather* is elite. And as I said, you must be a VIP or have a referral to enter.

Thankfully, I have Dr. Kizer's referral.

I slow my car as I approach the front circular driveway. Standing at the bottom of the large sweeping steps is a man in a dark gray uniform. While I usually notice a man in uniform, it's his other accessory that catches my attention. He's wearing a mask. It's black and covers his nose with openings for his eyes, a simple party mask. I suddenly recall Dr. Kizer's instructions. All visitors are to arrive prepared with a form of facial covering, something to keep everyone in attendance anonymous.

Bringing my car to a stop, I roll down my window.

The gentleman doesn't say a word, only reaches for the door handle to help me exit my car and enter *Lace and Leather*.

My voice quakes. "Um, I'm sorry. I forgot..."

His full lips straighten as he nods. His voice is deep and his enunciation and timbre practiced to the point of perfection. "We've been expecting you."

I blink up at his thick neck and broad shoulders. "Maybe another—"

"This is your first time," he says, not as a question.

Undoubtedly, my trembling grip of the steering wheel and my lack of preparedness all help with his assessment. And then I realize it was the code I was sent, the one I entered. It would make sense that the security for *Lace and Leather* knows the code of each entering patron.

"It is." *My first time.* I wave him off. "And it seems that I'm not prepared. Not to worry, I'll come back another time."

Reaching into the pocket of his jacket, he removes a piece of white satin. "White is for first timers. Next time, you will be prepared."

My pulse increases.

That didn't seem like a suggestion.

I fight the urge to reply. *Yes, Sir. I will be.*

"I-I um..."

He opens the car door and offers me his large gloved hand. "Welcome to *Lace and Leather*. Our first-time guests are special. I believe Dr. Kizer sent you."

Again, he isn't questioning.

"Yes, she did." As I stand on my high heels, my pulse kicks up even further until my knees wobble. I grip his hand tighter as the skirt of my black dress flutters lightly in the summer breeze. "Honestly, I'm not sure anymore if I should stay."

"I'll show you to Dorothy." With his other hand, he lifts the white satin. "First, you must put this on. I can help." His grin grows. "Unless you've changed your mind and plan to leave."

Peering upward at the majestic mansion, I take in the warm golden glow shining from the windows as the sound of jazz music infiltrates the night air. "Will I...what if...I change my mind?"

"Dorothy will show you around. You are free to leave at any time."

Inhaling, I nod, let go of his hand, and turn away, showing him the back of my head. "Okay, please put on the blindfold."

"It's not a blindfold. Here at *Lace and Leather* we encourage you to use your senses. Sight is a powerful sense." He eases the white satin over my eyes. Sewn openings fit perfectly over my eyes as the satin covers the top of my nose.

Except that it is white and tied in the back, it covers me as his mask does him.

After it is secured, the gentleman again offers me his hand. "Let me escort you up the stairs. The masks take a while to get used to wearing."

I place my hand in his, aware of how small I feel next to him. "Do you...? Are you...?"

"Not tonight, ma'am. I'm working."

I nod. "Okay. Thank you."

My shoulders straighten as he opens the door inward. *This is it...*

MARJI

*B*efore I can change my mind, I'm greeted. Standing at the ready is a pretty woman with red hair, wearing a black mask studded with rubies. "Welcome to *Lace and Leather*, I'm Dorothy."

"I'm..." I recall now that the instructions—the ones that mention bringing a mask—also say to use a pseudonym. I'm drawing a blank. And then I recall I spoke to my twin sister this afternoon. While I am certain she wouldn't be pleased I would use her name for a BDSM club, I am also sure she'll never know. Regaining a bit of composure, I offer my hand. "I'm Moira."

"Very nice, Moira. It's unusual for Dr. Kizer to refer singles to our club."

"She said..." I don't know how to finish that sentence since in reality, she didn't send me.

Dorothy's hand comes up. "Unusual, not unheard of. We have opportunities for singles and couples alike." She looks down at a paper in her hand. "I'll give you a tour based on the questionnaire Dr. Kizer asked that you complete."

My neck straightens.

I agonized over that questionnaire. It is probably easier to complete when planning this outing with a special someone. It is also probably easier when Dr. Kizer encourages desires and exploration. I neither have a special someone nor did I complete the questionnaire with Dr. Kizer's assistance.

"Okay," I say. "If I try something and then change my opinion, is the questionnaire set in stone?"

"Not at all, Moira. *Trying* is what is encouraged. There's no right or wrong, only trying."

That sounds similar to what Dr. Kizer says.

The entry where we are standing is separated from the main building. In its heyday it was probably a breeze-way, a place to keep cool air or warm from entering the main part of the house. As Dorothy opens the large wood door, the music from before becomes louder. Stepping inside, I turn my head to see all around.

Before us is a grand sweeping staircase similar to something out of a movie about a Southern plantation. Each room or hallway around the entry is isolated with large wooden pocket doors, yet the area doesn't appear small.

"In there," Dorothy points to the closest large doors, "is the bourbon bar. Once our tour is complete, if you'd like to get a drink or mingle, that is the place."

"Do people meet in there?"

"Yes. It's a chic yet comfortable atmosphere." She peers down at my black dress and tall heels. The dress is low-cut and the bodice hugs my breasts. The waist is tight but the skirt flows, falling to just above my knees.

It is an outfit I rarely wear, yet from what I've heard about *Lace and Leather*, it seems appropriate.

She smiles. "You're perfectly dressed. We encourage more formal attire. It seems these days that everyone is casual. Unless you come in knowing your partner or partners, we work to maintain a level of anonymity. That encourages freedom to participate without fear of seeing the other person on the street or at PTO."

I inhale again. "Does that work?"

"Quite well. Now, follow me."

Step by step, we ascend the staircase until we are on the second floor. "Up here are our private rooms."

My stomach begins to twist. "Dorothy, maybe...I don't know..."

"According to your questionnaire, you were interested in seeing." She smiles reassuringly. "Viewing. Tonight, Moira, is about seeing and being seen. Your white mask indicates that you are new. No one will expect anything more than you're willing to do. You also indicated that you don't believe you are interested in being paired with a couple."

My head shakes. "No...I don't..."

Dorothy stops walking. "You also indicated you believe you are submissive."

I swallow the lump in my throat. I haven't spoken aloud about these things to anyone, not Dr. Kizer or anyone, and yet here I am. Instead of answering, I nod.

"Have you ever acted upon those beliefs?"

I shake my head.

"Then the night is young. Perhaps you're not submissive. Perhaps you're a Dominant."

I feel my eyelashes against the satin as my eyes open wider. "I-I don't...I'm not sure I would know how."

Dorothy's smile broadens. "There are no rules other than respect. No matter which role you choose to try, remember everything is consensual. Safe words are established between individuals. In the meantime, no means no." Leading me down a hallway, she stops at a door. "This is a viewing room." She nods. "Are you still comfortable with viewing?"

"A couple?"

"Yes."

"Do they know I'm watching?"

"They hope someone is."

I take a deep breath as she opens the door inward.

"Come in, Moira."

The room around me is darkened, yet my eyes quickly adjust. To one side is a sofa as well as a table with two chairs. At the far end is a large chair and darkness. My mind is aflutter with what happens in this room.

Suddenly, the room fills with the sound of buzzing, yet I recall from what I've read that cell phones are strictly forbidden.

"I apologize," Dorothy says, lifting what appears to be an old-fashioned beeper. "I'm needed downstairs for a moment. Let me show you how to view and I'll be back in a few minutes."

"Show me?"

"Over here," she says, leading me to a remote control lying upon the table. "With this, you can illuminate the window before you. Rest assured that the couple within is aware they may be watched. It is only with the participants' permission that we would offer such a service."

My nose scrunches. "And they're okay with it?"

Dorothy's smile grows. "There is something liberating, empowering, and downright tantalizing in knowing you're being seen, that what you're doing is not only affecting you and your partner, but others as well." She hands me the remote. "It works mostly like a television remote. You can adjust the clarity of the vision as well as the volume."

"Can they see me?"

"No." Her head shakes. "Only if you want them to see you."

Trying to stay composed, I look down at the remote. "What is it like to be watched?"

Dorothy smiles. "Your questionnaire indicated you could enjoy it."

"But I'm alone."

"You're a beautiful woman about to watch something you've never seen in person. If you say no, then no one will watch you watch."

Watch me watch.

"I'm afraid I may not be of much interest."

"Is that a no?"

I shrug and take the remote from her hand into my shaky grasp. "It's not a no, which I suppose is a yes." My cheeks rise with the knowledge that I made my first decision of the night. "Will I know if someone is watching?"

"Only if that person wants it known."

I tug on my painted lip with my front teeth. "I guess if the person doesn't like what he sees, he won't let me know."

"That isn't always the case. Some voyeurs want to stay that way." She looks down at the remote. "See that blue button. It would allow you to speak to the room you're viewing."

My eyes open wide again. "I-I..."

"Exactly, not speaking doesn't mean you don't approve. Again, Moira, take tonight one moment at a time. Don't overthink. Tonight is special."

"Special?"

"You will never be here for your first time again."

I nod. "You're right." I look up at her ruby-studded mask. "You'll be back?"

She grins. "I'll knock first."

Taking a deep breath, I watch as Dorothy disappears behind the closing hallway door. Sitting on the edge of the sofa, I press my knees together and look down at the remote. I've watched porn.

This is the same, right?

LUCAS

I secure the black mask over my eyes as I pull my car up to *Lace and Leather*. It's been over two years since I last entered this establishment. When I did, Beth was beside me. We hadn't met here. No, I'd been a regular before meeting her. I never imagined a place like this would be her thing until Dr. Kizer encouraged us to be open with one another. Although we didn't meet here, our relationship had grown here. I wish there was another place to go, one that didn't hold memories of her. That is probably why I haven't been able to enter or even consider visiting.

It wasn't until after I ran into Dr. Kizer's assistant that I even began entertaining the idea of trying to rediscover my dominant side. Not that it was her, the assistant, who brought back those thoughts although I keep recalling the way she smiled at Callie instead of being annoyed. No, she simply reminded me that I'd been a patient of Dr. Kizer's.

While I wasn't ready to see the doctor, I finally got the courage to call. Thankfully, I had her private number, the one she'd shared with me after Beth's death.

Obviously, my lack of courage shows that my dominant side left with my wife.

For some reason, it had taken me years to make the call. Once I did, we spoke for a while. She listened and recommended that I reexplore my thoughts and desires.

She asked me to investigate my feelings, saying that if I'm not happy with where I am, perhaps I should remember what brought me happiness in the past and made me feel fulfilled.

Callie brings me happiness, but even so, I still feel like there's a part of me that is missing. According to Dr. Kizer, before I could rectify that emptiness, I needed to recognize what's missing—what would make me feel fulfilled. She suggested that once I determine the missing element, I should simply remind myself of what it was like.

That is why I'm here tonight.

Part of me fears that a reminder will do the opposite; instead of rekindling that desire, being here will confirm that my sense of control died the day Beth's car was struck by a distracted driver. It was sudden and there was nothing I could do to stop the chain of events. Perhaps that experience caused me to also lose my dominant nature. Maybe that part of my nature was buried along with the love of my life.

Or just maybe—and it's a long shot—as Dr. Kizer said, Beth loved life too much to want me to stop living. Whether it's at *Lace and Leather* or an Italian restaurant, I owe it to the love we shared to work my way out of my self-imposed isolation and try to remember how to live.

"Mr. Santana."

I straighten my shoulders. Mr. Santana is the name I used years ago. Hearing it without a missus sounds wrong. "Jonathon," I say to the man inside the entrance.

"Sir, it's nice to see you again."

My gaze moves about the familiar entry. "It's nice to be back."

That isn't a lie. Just stepping through the heavy wooden doors fills me with something that's been absent. There's a sense of power and an aura of control that permeates the air of *Lace and Leather*.

"Sir, would you like to enter the bourbon bar for your customary drink?"

Sir.

It's a customary greeting and yet within these walls it holds much more significance. With each reminder of *Lace and Leather*, my neck straightens and my circulation increases speed.

"Yes, I would like that."

A few moments later, I'm sitting at the shiny mahogany bar, taking in the recognizable sights and smells. Like a good cigar, the air is rich with scents.

Before me the bar is well stocked with only the top labels. The only thing missing would be the customary mirrored backdrop. Mirrors only appear at *Lace and Leather* for intimate purposes.

"Sir, what can I do for you?" The petite brunette is wearing a tight red dress, its bodice pulled tight pushing her small breasts upward, and her eyes shine through the openings of a black lace mask. Black lace on a woman means she's not only a server, but is also a member when she so desires.

"Two fingers of Blanton's, neat."

"Coming right up."

A few moments later, she's setting the crystal tumbler in front of me. "Sir, it's good to see you back. I don't know if you remember me. I'm Savannah, and I would be honored to welcome you back to *Lace and Leather* myself."

Not only isn't she my type, she's far too eager for my taste.

That isn't to mean I want an unwilling partner. I enjoy trepidation. I thrive on the endorphins that come about when the submissive relinquishes her fears and replaces them with trust. "Thank you, Savannah." We both know that isn't her real name. "Tonight, I'm just checking out the changes." I sighed. "And what has stayed the same."

"Yes, Sir. If you change your mind, I'm here."

"If I do, I'll let you know."

"Mr. Santana."

I turn toward the familiar woman's voice as a smile curls my lips. "Dorothy. I see you are still here."

"Every night." Her long eyelashes bat through her ruby-studded mask. "I prefer the nights I'm not working."

A scoff comes from my throat.

The ruby studs indicate she likes it particularly rough. If I were to guess, her nights of *not working* are in reality a lot of work. Accepting the sting of a cane or slashes of a bullwhip is both physical and mental exertion. While that degree of domination isn't my thing, I have utter respect for both the Dominants and submissives who enjoy that lifestyle.

"Oh, I can't fool you," she says. "It's good to see you back. Tonight it's my job to be sure our VIP guests are satisfied. Tell me, Sir, what will that take or who?"

I shake my head. "Dorothy, tonight is..." I'm not certain how to finish the sentence.

"Mr. Santana, *Lace and Leather* is at your disposal. Feel free to wander. Off-limit rooms are locked." She grinned. "Everything else is purposely accessible."

"I believe I will take a moment and enjoy my bourbon."

"The night is young," she says, handing me a card. "Before you were married, you were one of the best Doms with the new submissives." She nods toward the card. "It's her first time. No pressure, but she's upstairs."

As Dorothy walks away, I look down at the card in my hand. It contains no personal information. It is simply white with a room number. White means a novice. The idea intrigues me.

Maybe I could simply look in on her.

Instead of taking the main staircase, I enter the VIP hallway and push the button for the private elevator. The scissor type door opens as a uniformed man I don't recognize nods.

"Floor, Sir?" he asks.

I take one more look at the card. "Two."

We don't say another word as the elevator moves upward. Once the gate is opened, I slip into the VIP hallway that leads behind the private rooms. Each room has its own private rear viewing room, an area where rooms may be viewed singularly or as a couple. The one I entered has only one chair. It's leather and large, the kind of furniture that radiates respect, a throne of types, more like those seen in modern-day CEO offices, not ancient throne rooms.

Entering, I bypass the chair and go directly to the window. Pressing the button, the one that brings the darkened room into view, I place my fists on the windowsill and lean forward.

At first glance, I note that the woman inside the room, in the black dress and white mask is beautiful. I could imagine her to be the woman from the supermarket if I tried. She has long blonde hair that cascades over her bare shoulders. Her posture is straight, her sights set on the scene unfolding in the window before her. Every few seconds, she squirms, her body reacting to what she's seeing. I take in each movement, the way her nipples tent the bodice of her dress as her breasts heave. My gaze lowers and I notice the way the hem of her skirt is balled in her grip, showing her shapely legs. Her feet within high-heeled shoes fidget, sliding upon the hard surface flooring. It's as her lips open that my dick remembers what it's capable of doing.

"What are you watching, beautiful? Is it the first time you've watched real people?"

My questions are not audible. Yet with each passing second, my bloodstream flows, coursing faster through my veins, reminding me why I first found *Lace and Leather*.

Is it possible that there's hope?

Could I come back to life?

Back to life.

I ponder the thought as the blonde continues to bunch the hem of her black skirt, pulling it higher, exposing more and more of her thighs.

Life.

Maybe it is time to remember what that means.

MARJI

*a*fter the door shuts, I sit for a moment in the dark room alone.

There is no one to keep me here and no lock upon the door. It is my chance to leave *Lace and Leather* and never look back. The thought appears and just as quickly vanishes. I've made it this far and I don't want to turn back, not yet.

Call it curiosity...or maybe, work research.

That sounds reasonable.

I simply want to experience what I transcribe or at least see it.

Slowly, I convince myself to turn on the window and peer through the glass. After all, Dorothy said the couple wants to be seen. They want it. I recognize the fabrication I'm contriving to justify my presence. The truth is that I could call this research; however, as the tightening of my stomach continues to twist and the ache between my legs becomes more apparent, I admit that being here is more than research or even curiosity.

I *want* to see and to discover the world I've only heard about, only transcribed others' thoughts and feelings about.

I want to find out what it's like.

As my hand trembles, I lift the remote and click the button—not the blue button—the one that brings the window to life.

Such as on a television, the scene before me illuminates, coming into view. There are two people, a man and a woman. They're wearing masks.

Do they know one another?

Are they married?

Are they patients of Dr. Kizer's?

Do I know them?

My questions fade as my breath catches. None of that matters. I'm mesmerized by the intensity of their stares. Even with masks covering part of their faces, the connection they share is evident in the way the man is looking at the woman and the way she's looking at him. They may want to be viewed, but that isn't their prime concern. Their expressions mirror thoughts I've transcribed.

There is no one else in the world, no concern other than the other person.

The man is taller, his wide chest bare, yet his hips and long legs are covered by tailored black trousers. The woman on the other hand is mostly nude, wearing only a black lace bra and thong.

His lips move, yet I can't hear. The lack of sound doesn't diminish the visible authority in his body language.

I click another button and my dark room fills with this man's deep, dominating timbre. "I told you to wear red."

My heart thumps as his voice rumbles through my being. He isn't even talking to me, yet I feel his tone and cadence.

"I-I'm sorry. I forgot," the woman says, her eyes no longer staring upward but now veiled by her long lashes as her head bows, her chin falling near her chest.

The man reaches for her chin, lifting her eyes to him. "Have you also forgotten your manners when you address me?"

Her head shakes. "No, Sir. I'm sorry, Sir."

"You *forgot*. That is your excuse? Are you saying I'm not memorable—forgettable?"

"No, Sir. I-I just...forgot."

Behind the two of them is a four-poster bed covered by a red satin comforter. The room is painted a dark gray. In appearance, it's like any other bedroom in any other house. I suck in a breath and sit taller as the man instructs the woman to remove her black panties and place her hands and chest on the bed, reminding her that he wanted red and that's what he's going to get.

I squeeze my thighs together, watching, as he reaches for the buckle of his belt.

Holy crap. He's going to punish her.

I bite my lower lip as my neck straightens. I've read about this from the female clients in Dr. Kizer's practice. I've read their thoughts of appreciation of submission and their desire for firm boundaries.

Intellectually, it seems wrong to not only accept this treatment, but desire it.

Desire isn't intellectual.

It's not a thought process.

Dr. Kizer reminds her clients of that. She says not to overthink—to feel.

It makes sense in the abstract, yet her notes are different. They are simply words on a recording. This before me is more—intense, real, and just... more.

I'm not only hearing it. I am seeing it, their expressions, their nonverbal communication, and their peace and contentment.

It is said that a picture is worth a thousand words. If I were to take a picture of what I'm seeing, I am not sure I could put the powerful emotions into words.

It's their shared total acceptance that takes my breath away.

The woman doesn't protest, doing exactly as she is told.

The man isn't angry or upset.

I'm swept up in the scene.

It's sensual, sexy, and utterly compelling.

Both of these people are exactly where they want to be, doing what they want to do.

And all at once, I gasp and my body flinches.

I'd been too wrapped up to notice him removing his belt when the leather slices through the air.

A whistle and a crack.

The sound reverberates through my darkened room, prickling my skin as the leather makes contact with hers.

"Oh!" I call out. Yet the other woman through the window doesn't make a sound. While her hands ball and she fists the comforter beneath her, her only other movement appears to be one of relief. Instead of tensing, her muscles relax. Her spine pushes toward the bedding and her legs spread giving both of us a view of her most sensitive parts.

There's another lash and then another.

I fidget upon the sofa, imagining the sensation on my backside. My head shakes, wondering how many more she can take. While her skin displays the evidence of his punishment, it's her increased squirming that has both his and my attention.

The man pauses, lowering the belt to the floor, and rubs his palm over his artistic creation. With the concentration of a blind man reading Braille, he touches each raised, angry lash mark.

The woman looks back, craning her head over her shoulder as tears stream down her cheeks, yet she remains mute.

I shouldn't be enthralled. I shouldn't be turned on.

My core shouldn't be growing wet and my breasts heavy. None of that should be happening, yet it is.

"Will you remember next time?" he asks.

"Yes, Sir." When he doesn't respond, she adds, "Please, Sir."

I squeeze my legs together tighter, feeling her unspoken request twisting inside me.

He teases her tender skin, dipping closer and closer to her core. "You begged. Tell me, what you are begging for?"

I hold my breath as I wait for her answer—the one I know.

"Please, Sir, I'm needy."

The man grins. "Only good girls get to come."

"I won't forget again."

"I'm not certain I believe you."

"I won't," she says, her voice now cracking with emotion as her head shakes.

I have the urge to get up, go out in the hallway, open their door, go inside that room, and plead her case. Yet like her, I'm paralyzed, unable to move away from where I'm seated.

The man unlatches her black bra. He guides her to stand and spins her around. Dropping the bra to the floor, he asks, "These tits..." His lips curl upward into a menacing grin as he tweaks each nipple. "...what color?"

"Red, Sir." She blinks and winces yet remains facing him, willing and ready for whatever he has planned.

Tipping his chin toward the bed, he delivers his next command.

Swallowing, I reach for the hem of my black dress as the woman climbs onto the bed, purposely lying on her back and dragging her wounded backside over the blanket below. The infinitesimal flinches are the only indication that she's tender, yet again, she doesn't complain.

The man steps away and then reappears with a long leather crop.

I cringe as the air fills with the sound of a slap, and the crop comes down hard on one breast and then the other.

Reflexively, I reach up, covering my own. It's as if I'm there, not only watching, but also experiencing the pain. It's then I realize I've lifted the hem of my dress and my knees are no longer together, but spread...giving me access...

Suddenly, a window I thought was a mirror lights in the back of the room.

Startled, I turn toward the light and gasp.

Through the glass is a dark-haired man, wearing a dark suit, white shirt, and charcoal-gray tie. The way the suit is tailored and with the coat open, his broad shoulders and trim waist are accentuated. My teeth tug on my lower lip as I take him in, for a moment wondering if he's real.

He leans forward, appearing taller and more menacing. His black mask is inches from the window. I'm drawn to the dark eyes peering through the openings and their intensity as they stare at me.

"Keep going," he says, his voice deeper than the man in the other room, more commanding.

"I-I...*going?*" I say, unsure of what he means or what's even happening.

"You want to touch yourself. Do it."

I peer down at my dress now bunched near the top of my thighs as my heart pounds against my chest. It's not like I haven't done this before—pleasured myself. It's that I've never done it with someone watching or commanding my next move.

"You were given an order. Do you know what happens when you disobey?"

My eyes move from the man to the couple.

I do know. I am still seeing her punishment.

"I-I..." My tongue feels dry as I try to form words.

"The answer is 'yes, Sir, or no, Sir.' Do you know?"

"Yes, Sir."

LUCAS

For a moment, her startled doe-eyed stare peering my way makes me wonder if Dorothy was right, that this woman agreed to instruction and to being viewed. There is no doubt that Dorothy was correct about this beautiful woman's status. The white satin mask isn't the only clue that this gorgeous creature is in a new element. Her piquing interest and wanton needs emanate from her. It's as if even through the glass I can smell her desire.

I tilt my chin. "Lie back against the arm of the sofa so I can see."

Her head moves from side to side. "What?"

My neck tightens. "Tell me what part of my instructions was unclear." My tone deepens with each word.

She doesn't speak as she looks around as if she had forgotten where she was. Move by move, she complies, laying her head upon the arm at the far end of the sofa.

Her lovely long hair flows in soft waves over her bare shoulders and the way her nipples protrude, tenting the material as her breasts heave under her dress, I'm certain she isn't wearing a bra.

I wait as the situation settles over her. It's like watching a kitten whose eyes have just opened. The world it's only heard is now present and real. The enormity of her first time hits me.

Even after all of this time, Dorothy believes I can still do this, that I'm the man for the job.

As the woman's eyes return to me, I know I want to be that man.

The woman glances toward her feet still on the floor and back to me. While I am turned on by her trepidation, I need words. When she doesn't speak, I do.

"Lift them, gorgeous. Keep the shoes on. One higher on the back of the sofa with the other knee bent outward."

More shallow breaths and I worry this little doe may hyperventilate before I see what I want to see.

"Breathe."

Nodding, she slowly moves her legs to where I said. As she does, I am struck by the shapeliness of her calves and tone of her muscles. I want to ask if she's a runner. I want to ask about the way she spends her time and what she enjoys. I want to know why she's alone.

My gaze goes to her hands, fluttering near her face with her elbows bent. There's no ring to indicate she belongs to another man.

Why are you alone, beautiful?

I don't ask any of my questions—that isn't what this is about. Dorothy sent me in here to usher this beautiful creature into a world she may have imagined but has never experienced. If I were to face the truth, Dorothy also sent me in here for me to welcome myself back.

Though I want this lovely woman's eyes on me, I direct otherwise. "Turn, beautiful, look back through the window at what you were watching."

At first, she hesitates as her red lip disappears beneath her front teeth, and then she complies, showing me the perfection of her profile, her upturned nose, high cheekbones, and slender neck. When her gaze meets the window, she sucks in a breath.

At least she's breathing.

Oh, how I wish I could see two rooms, to know what she's seeing; however, from my angle it's impossible. Even the audible is indistinguishable through two speakers.

"Tell me what you see," I command.

Her lips press together as she returns her stare to me. "I-I..."

"Yes, Sir. No, Sir."

"Yes, Sir."

Her arms reach higher until they're over her head and she's holding her own hand. I want those hands on her body. I want to watch as she brings herself pleasure, but first, I need to return her thoughts to the room next door.

"Eyes toward the window."

Even with the white satin mask limiting my view, I can see her long lashes bat, and she fixes her gaze on the other couple.

"Oh!" she exclaims, her soft voice filled with emotion. "The...crop is gone."

Oh fuck.

There was a crop.

How long has it been...?

"Why was there a crop?" I ask, knowing the answer and wanting to hear her verbalize it.

"The man...he said he told the woman to wear red."

"She disobeyed." The thought causes blood to rush to my growing dick. "What did he do?"

Her gaze is now unwavering upon the window.

"He punished her." Her breathing is accelerating and her hands seem to tremble. "First with a belt and then the crop. Now, he's denying her..."

A warm sense of power flows through me. It's one of the best punishments. Submissives willingly take the lash of a belt or crop. They'll accept clamps to even their most sensitive areas. They'll do whatever is commanded knowing relief is their reward.

Denying submissives the pleasure of an orgasm is their greatest fear, the punishment that stays with them the longest. In a long-term relationship, that punishment can be extended over hours or days until her need is all she can think about, until it's something she is willing to do anything to receive.

"Tell me what she wants," I say.

"She hasn't said," the woman pants, her eyes wide on the scene.

"What do you think she wants?"

"Him, inside her. She wants to be satisfied."

"He's not going to give it to her."

Her eyes flash my direction and the light catches them just right. They're the most brilliant light shade of blue, warm and pleasing while simultaneously curious and alarmed.

"Did I tell you to look my way?"

Her head shakes as she turns back to the window. "No, Sir. Sorry, Sir. He's telling her to kneel."

Her immediate response gives my dick a zap of electricity. "What do *you* want?"

"I want what he won't give her."

"You want that man inside you?"

"No," she responds quickly, keeping her eyes toward the window. "I want the satisfaction he's denying her."

"Are you wet?"

She quickly nods.

My neck straightens. "Spread those sexy legs. Lift your dress and show me."

As she complies, I see that she's not bare under her dress. She's wearing the tiniest lace panties. The small black lace triangle barely covers her pussy, revealing that she also isn't shaved. Instead she has what appear to be soft blonde curls.

Fuck.

This woman couldn't be more perfect if I'd called ahead and ordered the woman of my desires.

"Take off the panties. I want to see you."

"I've never—"

"Yes, Sir. No, Sir," I remind her, interrupting.

She reaches down to the waistband and lowers the black lace over her hips. As she lifts her ass from the sofa, she replies, "Yes, Sir."

The black lace lowers over her shapely legs and her high-heeled shoes until it's free. She drops it to the floor. Inch by inch she opens herself, revealing the soft yellow curls and needy pink pussy.

Perhaps it's because I haven't done anything like this in so long. Maybe it's this woman's desire mixed with trepidation. I didn't want to analyze. Nevertheless, I can't remain where I am. Turning the knob of the door beside the window, I step into the room with the blonde-haired beauty. The room is filled with deep moans of pleasure combined with gasps, letting me know that while the woman next door isn't being satisfied, the man is.

The blonde-haired beauty's gaze snaps to me.

Without speaking, I walk to her, my steps determined yet slow, my shoes tapping upon the hard surface until I'm towering over her curves and exposed sex. I reach out my hand. "Give me the remote."

Without looking away or speaking, with her blue eyes wide and staring up at me, she reaches down, fumbling until she finds the remote and hands it my direction.

Never turning toward the window, I darken the scene and quell the sound.

I should go back to the chair in the viewing room. Or even to the chair in this room. I can't. Now that I'm so close to her, I can't move away.

This could be against her request. I didn't ask. I'd agreed to command from afar. However, there's something drawing me to her. I have to touch her.

Reaching for her chin, I tilt her beautiful face my direction. "Don't look away."

"Yes, Sir."

I hold her soft, warm skin in my grasp. While maintaining my deep tone, I reassure her. "Do as I say and you'll get what you want."

She swallows. "Yes, Sir. I'll do as you say."

"Touch yourself."

I don't have to tell her where. Immediately one of her hands lowers to her pussy as the other grips the skirt of her dress.

"Are you wet?" I ask as her fingers graze over her clit before spreading herself open and teasing her entrance.

"Yes, Sir. I am."

I lower my face to hers. We're inches apart as her chin trembles in my grasp, yet her blue eyes never leave mine. "I am going to direct your next moves. You'll listen to my voice only. If you're a good girl and obey, you will have the best orgasm of your life. If you are *very* good, we both will. If you don't want to comply, tell me now, and we will both walk away from here. Yes, Sir. Or no, Sir."

MARJI

"Yes, Sir. Or no, Sir."

Dorothy's words come back to me. Couples establish their own safe words, but in the meantime, remember that no means no. This man is giving me that out. This man I don't know, the one who instructed me to remove my underwear and has seen my core, not only seen but has watched as I touched myself.

Trust.

That is what Dr. Kizer says is needed.

Is it possible to trust a man I don't even know?

"Sir?" I ask, my chin still in his grasp.

His chin raises as his dark eyes penetrate my barriers. "Yes, Sir. No, Sir."

"If I say no, Sir...?"

"I told you, beautiful, what will happen either way."

He did. We walk away, or if I say yes, the best orgasm of my life is within reach.

Reaching up, I take his hand, the one holding my chin. Our gazes stay fixed upon one another. "Yes, Sir," I say as our fingers intertwine. "I trust you."

His gaze goes to where our hands are touching. "Stand up, beautiful. If we're both getting what we want, the dress needs to come off."

Come off.

There should be alarm bells ringing. There should be fear flushing my bloodstream. There should be concern over being with someone I don't know and may never see again. All of those things *should be* happening. Instead, our hands rotate until mine is laid in his and he helps me stand. Even with me in my heels, this man is much taller than I. Not only tall, he is broad and his shoulders are wide. Though his tone has softened, there is still dominance in his voice and actions. He is allowing my refusal while at the same time doing as he'd said and directing my movements.

Spinning me, he unlatches the top of the bodice behind my neck. All at once the front of my dress falls forward revealing my breasts. Before unlatching the skirt, he spins me again. The rich aroma of his cologne mixes with the scent of bourbon filling my senses as the warmth of his closeness radiates against my exposed skin.

As we're now side by side, the man sweeps my long hair over my shoulders, all the while staring unabashedly at my breasts. Though he doesn't speak, I feel his gaze over my flesh until my nipples grow even harder.

The corners of his lips move upward as he keeps his gaze on my breasts, reaches behind me, unbuttons the skirt of the dress, and lowers the zipper. The entire dress flutters to the floor, creating a black puddle around my shoes.

Again my hand is in his.

"Back as you were."

Words of questioning come to mind, yet I keep them at bay, responding as he taught me. "Yes, Sir."

Once I'm lain back, my legs where he wants them, the shoes as he directs, and my hair flowing over the arm of the sofa, he again reaches for my hand and lowers it to my core.

"Think about what you saw. Did his punishment excite you?"

The scene comes back.

I nod.

His finger traces my painted lips. "You have a voice. Use it. I want to hear you. I want to hear your answers. If the time comes, I want to hear your pleas and your cries of ecstasy and pain. Speak."

Holy shit.

This is real.

This is happening and my body is on fire.

"Yes, Sir. It turned me on."

"Have you ever felt the bite of a belt?"

I begin to shake my head and quickly recover. "No, Sir."

"A crop?"

"A cane?"

I reply in the negative each time, yet the images are burnt into my mind as I imagine each implement stinging my flesh. My pussy clenches as my nipples continue to grow painfully hard.

He pushes my legs farther apart as he stares down at my core. I fight the urge to press my legs together, to hide what I'm certain he can see, that I'm wet with anticipation.

When he looks up and our gazes meet, his dark eyes gleam. "A crop to the tender flesh of a pussy is better than a jolt of electricity."

My eyes widen as my insides twist. The need to close my thighs and protect my most sensitive skin is almost unsurmountable as my knees flinch. "Electricity? A crop...there?"

Instead of answering, he continues his demands, "Keep your eyes on me and show me how you do it, how you make yourself come."

The idea of denying that I do this—touch myself—or have done it comes to mind. Instead, I stare into his dark gaze as I find my clit. Little circles to the sensitive nerves cause my neck to straighten and back to arch. I continue moving as I find my opening and confirm what I already knew. Using my essence, I continue to bring myself higher.

It isn't only my touch.

It's him. The intensity of his stare zeroed in on me.

It's his proximity as he watches my every move.

I have an unfamiliar need to please him with my compliance, and by the way his stare is darkening, I believe I am. That alone is enough to bring me to a climax. My own touch is simply extra.

It's as I moan that his hand reaches for mine. Lifting it, he opens his full lips and slowly sucks my essence from my fingers.

Holy shit, that's hot.

"Now your breasts," he demands.

I am too hypnotized by his deep voice, actions, the guttural sounds he makes, and his presence to argue. In the past, I have largely ignored my own breasts, instead concentrating on my relief and then moving on, usually going to sleep. Doing as he says, I lift both hands, finding that my breasts are heavier than normal.

"Pinch your nipples."

I let out a squeal, surprised by their sensitivity.

"Imagine that crop on them when they're as stunning and engorged as they are right now."

I can't imagine.

I've never considered it and now the image of the woman next door takes on more meaning. The man waited until she was hot and bothered to punish her breasts, knowing they would be more painful.

"Please, Sir," I plead, wanting more, just as she had.

The man reaches for the buckle of his belt.

What is he going to do?

It's then I notice the bulge, his growing erection. When my eyes widen under the satin, he says, "The rules haven't changed, beautiful."

I'm not sure what that means and yet no matter what it is, I'm not prepared to say no.

This man doesn't remove his belt as the man next door did. Instead, he unlatches it and then the top button of his trousers and lowers the zipper. It's as he pushes down the waistband of his boxer briefs that his erection springs forward.

I take it in, the length and girth. Perhaps it's my angle or maybe being at *Lace and Leather*, yet I want to reach out, to touch the velvety surface and lick the shiny tip.

His large hand palms his length.

"Make yourself come, but don't look away."

I don't know if he means from his sexy eyes or from his glorious penis. Either way, I can't look anywhere else as one of my hands tends to my tender breasts and the other circles my clit He continues his instructions dictating my rate, speeding me up and slowing me down. The experience is agony and ecstasy all in one. Highs and lows. Peaks and valleys. The sensations combine with his timbre, together winding my insides like an old-fashioned top until spinning out of control is my only option.

The room around us fills with noises—both his and mine. My back arches and the heels of my shoes threaten the sofa's leather surface.

I'm on the precipice when his hand upon his cock

speeds up and his face beneath the black mask contorts. I've never touched myself in front of a man nor have I watched as a man did the same. It's possibly the most sensual and sexual encounter I've ever had without having sex.

I'm not sure if I'm supposed to ask for permission to orgasm. To be honest, I can't even think about what is *supposed* to happen. My mind is a blur as my skin heats and every nerve in my body ignites. Such as a series of fireworks on a Fourth of July celebration, the fuse has been lit. There's no turning back.

"Oh! Oh!" Each of my proclamations is louder than the last.

My toes curl within the confines of the shoes as my legs involuntarily straighten.

A series of detonations occur, beginning in my core and radiating in all directions as my entire body erupts. I try to keep my eyes on him, yet my lids close as the explosions continue. I open my eyes as the room fills with a guttural roar and my stomach grows warm and wet.

It takes my hazy mind a moment to realize that I'm not the only one who's orgasmed. His hand continues to move up and down as a silky white stream coats my skin.

Obey and you'll have the best orgasm of your life. If you're very good, we both will.

His words bring a smile to my face.

I continue my stare of his hand over his large penis when all at once he pushes his still-hard cock away, hiding it behind the layers of material. His shoulders straighten and neck elongates. His dark gaze has lost the spark of earlier, deepening into the dominating stare from the man in the window.

Unsure what to do, I remain still as he walks into the shadows near the back of the room and emerges with tissues in hand. I hold my breath as he lowers himself, bending his knees and sitting upon his haunches, and slowly and methodically wipes away his seed, cleaning my skin.

My smile fades with uncertainty as I watch his every move. Though I believe I shouldn't say a word, I want to protest his care, to say that he's marked me and I don't want his mark gone. Once he's satisfied, he again offers me his hand. Taking it, I stand on wobbly legs as he lifts my dress from the floor and lays it gently onto the sofa.

"Do you have a name, gorgeous?" His deep voice speaks to my core like it did when he was directing my movements.

"Yes, Sir." My voice sounds different, more demure yet confident.

Is that possible after only one experience?

His cheeks rise as with one hand he lifts my chin, bringing our gazes together, and the other snakes around my waist, pulling my naked body against his clothed solid frame. "What is your name? Whom should I request upon my next visit?"

Next visit?

My pulse increases.

Did I plan to return?

His grip of my chin tightens as he raises it higher. "*No, Sir* is still an option."

I swallow, saying a silent apology to my sister. "My name is Moira, Sir. How will I know when the next time will be?"

"You'll be informed, Moira. Until then, remember what happened. Think about it. Dream about it."

I am certain I will not forget what happened—ever.

I nod, my breasts heaving as my heart thunders against his chest. The cologne cloud from before is now mixed with the lingering scent of our arousals.

"One more thing," he says. Not waiting for me to respond, he continues, "Do not touch yourself again." He releases my chin and reaches for my hand. "If these fingers..." His lips kiss the tips of the fingers I'd just used to touch myself. "...touch that perfect pussy, the next time we're together, your pussy will meet a crop before getting any opportunity for relief."

A crop.

There!

His neck straightens. "Come now, Moira. I'm waiting for your answer."

My answer?

A crop?

My mind is consumed with the idea.

I don't have an answer. I have questions.

And then it hits me, the answer he's waiting to hear.

"Yes, Sir."

"Yes, Sir...what?"

"I want there to be a next time and I won't..." Why is saying the words more embarrassing than doing the act?

"You won't touch yourself."

I nod. "Yes, Sir. I won't do that."

His lips curl in amusement. "You're precious."

"Is that bad? Did I do something wrong?"

"No, Moira, you are perfect."

Perfect.

How can one word fill me with such contentment?

His lips brush the top of my head as he releases me. Reaching for my dress, he stills as his gaze scans from my blonde hair to my shoes. "That body shouldn't be covered, but the idea of anyone else seeing you like this is strangely upsetting. Get dressed and wait. Don't leave this room alone. I'll send Dorothy to retrieve you and accompany you to your car."

"She suggested the bourbon bar?" I don't know what made me mention it. The truth is I'm too overwhelmed with what just occurred to enter a bar or meet more people.

His head shakes as his dark gaze narrows under the mask. "No."

"No?"

"Wait for Dorothy."

"Yes, Sir." I think about coming face-to-face with the woman who brought me here. As I do, my cheeks fill with heat. "Will she know what we...?"

"Being viewed by others may be approved by you, but

it's not by me. No one knows but us. Assumptions will be made based on *Lace and Leather*. However, only we know what occurred."

I let out a breath. "Thank you, Sir." Clutching my dress to my breasts, I stand enthralled with a man I barely know. And then it occurs to me. I don't know him at all. As he begins to walk away, I ask, "Sir, do you have a name?"

MARJI

*M*r. Santana.
Broad shoulders.
Commanding timbre.
Full lips.
Dark, penetrating stare.
The feel of those lips on my hair and fingers makes me want them on other places, makes my skin yearn for more.

I wake from my restless sleep covered in perspiration as my hand snakes down my stomach and my fingers tease the waistband of my underwear. These aren't made of lace. These are ones I've had for years, boy shorts made of cotton. And as my dream fades—the one of Mr. Santana sitting on the chair in the darkened room directing my movements, his deep voice commanding the removal of my dress, leaving nothing but the lace thong and high heels, and telling me to come to him, not on my feet, but crawling on my knees—reality sets in.

I'm not at *Lace and Leather*. I haven't been there since last Saturday night. It's now nearly Thursday morning, and I've heard nothing from the man who said I'd be informed about our next meeting nor from Dorothy or anyone else at the club.

My hand stills as I stare up at the ceiling in my bedroom and watch the reflections of light from the outside lamps dance across the surface.

He told me to think about what happened. He told me to dream about it.

I'm not certain how one man can have that much influence, but with each passing minute, hour, and day what happened at *Lace and Leather* is all I can think about. It's unforgettable. Even at work, I have had to delete entire pages of notes as Dr. Kizer's dictations morph into my experience, morphing further into my fantasies.

I've told myself I would visit the club once, experience the things I've heard about, and be done.

That isn't what happened.

I want more.

I want so much more, and in every vision, every glimpse into my imagination, Mr. Santana is there with his dark eyes gleaming as a crop reddens my skin. I've been online as well as transcribed clients' thoughts. My mind knows that the leather will bite and yet despite the way my heart thumps in wary anticipation, I want to experience it. I want the pain because once he's done, I'll hear his voice. 'No, Marji, you're perfect.' And then that cock of his will take away the pain, bringing me pleasure that my own hands could never match.

My fingers move lower, under the waistband.

I suddenly realize the error in my fantasy. He doesn't know my real name. I don't know his.

"Come on, Marji," I say aloud to myself. "You're probably never going to hear from him again. What are you going to do, spend the rest of your life without satisfaction? How will he know?"

Exhaling, I pull my hand up to my chest and roll onto my stomach, keeping it pinned beneath me. If I placed a pillow beneath me and moved my hips, that isn't touching, is it?

His dark eyes appear and I know that he didn't forbid what I've imagined, yet it was implied. Sighing, I roll again, throwing the covers off only to wake minutes later with a chill and pull them back on.

This is agony.

"Saturday will be a week," I say aloud to the darkness. "Seven days. If I'm not informed by Saturday, I will take matters into my own hands."

I've given the idea of my information some thought. Since the club uses pseudonyms and the forms are filled out with identification numbers, how can I be informed? I even asked Dorothy that the night she came to retrieve me.

Letting out a long breath, I think back to her entrance.

. . .

NEARLY A WEEK AGO

Time has passed, yet I'm not sure of how long. The window across the room is still dark, the way Mr. Santana made it and now I'm wondering if the couple is still there. Did he let her come? Did he allow her any satisfaction?

A smile comes to my lips.

Did he mark her as I was marked?

I startle as the sound of knocking refocuses me. Standing, I smooth my dress and walk to the door. "Yes?"

"Moira, it's Dorothy. I was told you are ready to leave."

Taking one last look around the room, I make a mental note to remember everything about it, from the leather sofa to the large chair near the back and the table with chairs near the front. I said I'd return, but if I don't, I don't want to forget what happened.

I plaster a smile on my lips as I open the door. "Thank you, Dorothy, for coming to get me."

Behind her ruby-studded mask, her green eyes glisten and her painted lips part as her smile broadens. "We're happy you decided to join us tonight at Lace and Leather. *While it's getting late, the bourbon bar is still serving. Perhaps you'd enjoy a drink before you go?"*

I shake my head, recalling Mr. Santana's response when I mentioned the same thing. "No, thank you. I think I should go. Is my car accessible?"

"Are you sure, sweetie?" Dorothy asks as she lays a hand on my shoulder. "The first visit can be...well, let's just say a few fingers of good bourbon can calm the nerves."

The truth is that after that amazing orgasm, I'm about as

relaxed as one could get. That doesn't mean that the last few minutes or more that I was alone weren't nerve-racking. They were. Nevertheless, there was something in Mr. Santana's tone as he forbade a stop at the bar that lingers in my consciousness.

"Really," I say with all the confidence I can muster, "I'm ready to go."

"Very well." She releases my shoulder and reaches for my arm, weaving hers through my elbow. "Did you enjoy yourself?"

Though we're walking toward the staircase and no one else is about, I can't help but feel on display. "I did," I answer softly. At the top of the stairs, I stop and turn to her. "How...? He said...he'd request me."

Suddenly the sentence felt wrong, like I am an off-menu dinner special, a table at a fine restaurant, or more likely, a prostitute at a house of ill-repute.

Dorothy looks me in the eye. "Moira, you are a beautiful single woman. You may come back to Lace and Leather whenever you desire. There's no rule to stay monogamous. I am certain if you entered the bourbon bar tonight or another evening, you would have a list of willing candidates."

"But...if I wanted to stay...monogamous?"

Her lips pull tight. "Honey, if Mr. Santana makes a request for you, I can send you a text, if you allow me to have your number."

"Don't you already?"

"No. If Lace and Leather were to contact you, it would be through your referral. We keep no identifying personal information on hand."

My referral. Does that mean they'd contact Dr. Kizer?

"And if I give you my number, you won't share it?"

"No, dear. It's totally up to you."

I nod. *"I'd like to know if he requests me. He said he would."*

Her neck straightens. "Oh, he did?"

"Maybe it's just a line," I say, disheartened.

"Moira, listen to me. Mr. Santana doesn't need lines. There was a time when that man was the most sought-after Dom. He has a reputation that from all I've heard is not conceived of lore. If he didn't want to see you again, he wouldn't have made the comment."

"Then yes, please take my number."

THURSDAY MORNING

I wake as sunlight streams through my bedroom window. Filtering in from the outside is the melody of birds as I roll on the cool sheets. I must have finally fallen asleep and yet my first thought isn't of the morning or the sunlight. It's of him, of us, of what happened.

It's crazy because there have been men I've slept with —well, not slept but had sex with—who I didn't think this much about. Mr. Santana and I didn't have sex but then again, we had more.

I sigh as his dark eyes come to mind.

Lying on my back, I prop up my pillow and reach for my phone.

09:35 a.m.

Holy shit!

I'm late for work.

Kicking off the covers, I phone Dr. Ami Kizer. She answers on the first ring. "Dr. Kizer, this is Marji."

"Yes, Marji, my phone told me that. Is everything all right?"

"No. Shit. I'm sorry. I must have overslept. I just woke up." My mind is racing as I hurry toward my attached bathroom. "I'll be there by..." I think about the commute. "...a little after eleven at the latest. I'll try for sooner. I'm so very sorry."

Dr. Kizer laughs. "First oversleeping incident in over two years, no worries. Are you certain you're all right?"

Am I?

I'm hot and bothered and losing sleep over a man I don't even know.

Perfectly normal, right?

"I'm good." And then I recall her schedule. "You have Luke McAroy at ten and Mr. and Mrs. Jenson at eleven."

"I'll be fine."

"You can keep the phones going to the answering service," I offer. "I'll catch up as soon as I get in. I'm so sorry."

"Marji, calm down and get here as soon as you can."

"Thank you." I disconnect the phone call and sigh.

"Great time to oversleep, Marji," I say to myself. It's true. I was looking forward to seeing Luke McAroy again. A smile comes to my lips as I recall him at the supermarket with his adorable daughter, how amused he was with her, lighthearted, and caring. I was glad when Dr. Kizer told me he'd called her, even happier when I answered the phone to schedule this appointment. It is hard to imagine that great guy at the store followed Dr. Kizer's suggestions in the past. Maybe it was at his late wife's suggestion.

Turning on the shower, I turn and peer into the mirror over the sink. The image staring back has messy blonde hair and big dark circles beneath her eyes. "Yeah, you're perfect all right. A perfect mess.

"Maybe you should think about a real man like Luke and give up the fantasy of Mr. Santana?" I shrug. "At least then you could sleep."

Forty minutes later, dressed and ready for work with my long, wet hair braided over one shoulder, I grab my phone from the nightstand. It's then that I see that I have a text message.

It's probably from Dr. Kizer. That thought doesn't stop my pulse from increasing. I tap the icon and the message comes into view.

MOIRA, THIS IS DOROTHY. YOUR PRESENCE IS REQUESTED AT LACE AND LEATHER THIS FRIDAY NIGHT AT 8 P.M. MR. SANTANA WOULD LIKE TO SEND A MESSENGER WITH YOUR ATTIRE AND INSTRUCTIONS FOR THE EVENING. IF YOU AGREE TO MEET HIM ON HIS TERMS, PLEASE RESPOND WITH YOUR ADDRESS.

. . .

My knees give out as I sink to the edge of my unmade bed. He wants to see me again.

That's what I wanted, isn't it?

Shit, Friday is tomorrow.

His terms...what does that mean?

I reread the text message. He also wants my address.

Is that safe?

Do I trust him?

Shit.

LUCAS

J open the door to Dr. Kizer's office as a million memories bombard my thoughts. There are so many that I hesitate, unsure if I can enter. It's then that I see her; Dr. Kizer is sitting at the assistant's desk, Marji's.

I'm surprised by my twinge of disappointment. No matter how I try, I haven't been able to get Marji out of my mind, not since Callie and I ran into her—well, Callie literally ran into her—at the grocery store. And then there was Moira at *Lace and Leather* who also made me think of Marji. I guess I'd hoped that seeing her today would bring any questions or illusions of their resemblance to a close.

"Luke," Dr. Kizer says as she stands. "I'm so happy you decided to come see me."

"Are you doing your own front-office work now, Doctor? I could tell some others about your practice if things are slow."

She smiles. "I always accept referrals, but this isn't a statement on the practice. We're busy. It's only that Marji is running late." She gestures toward her office door. "Come on back. I have coffee brewing. It's not going to be as good as Marji's, but if you'd like a cup, we can get one before beginning your session."

My session.

The reality is that I almost didn't make this appointment. Once it was set, I almost didn't attend. After talking to Dr. Kizer on the phone, I did as she recommended and made a trip to *Lace and Leather*. I hadn't expected to enjoy myself. I half expected that any remaining tendencies I possessed toward domination would be gone. I thought I could enter the bourbon bar and basically toast to the loss of a lifestyle that was no longer.

What I sure as hell didn't expect to do was to meet a first-timer who would sweep me off my feet.

When I told Moira that I would request her, I'd been sincere. It was all I could think to say as she stared up at me with those mesmerizing blue orbs, wide and staring at me from behind her white mask, her pert red lips, and her warm, nude body against me. It was her fucking first time, and she couldn't have been more perfect, more genuine, or more trusting. She hit every damn button and checked every box on my list of desires, even ones I'd thought no longer existed.

Then I spent all day Sunday with Callie, doing everything to get Moira off my mind. We went out for pancakes. We went to the zoo and then to the aquarium. It was as I offered a movie that my four-year-old set me straight. "Daddy, I want to go home. It was fun at Grandma and Grandpa's and the pancakes with straws-berries and the animals and fishies. I'm tired. Can't we go home?"

She was right.

Without understanding in her four-year-old mind, she told me to face what I didn't want to see. It's one thing to be a single dad out and about. It's another to be that person in our own house, one that suddenly feels emptier.

Throughout the day, I'd been trying to hide from the truth that lurks in our home, the truth that becomes reality once Callie is asleep. I'm lonely for the compan-ionship of an adult. It was one thing to feel that way in the abstract; it is quite another thing when that emotion is accompanied by a tantalizing masked face and a sexy-as-hell body with a willingness to try the unknown.

Going home, I came to realize that I'd been trying to keep my mind occupied and not think about the gorgeous submissive who graced my presence as well as my dreams the night after our encounter.

Avoidance is exhausting and Callie was right.

That didn't mean I was willing to face Moira again.

Monday, Tuesday, and even Wednesday I told myself it wasn't real. And yet each time my eyes closed, I saw her big blue doe-eyes staring at me. I recalled her reaching for my hand and telling me, a man she didn't know, that she trusted me. I remembered the taste of her from the tips of her fingers.

Finally, late last night after assuring that my parents were up for another sleepover, I called Dorothy at *Lace and Leather*. If I am going to be the one who brings Moira into this lifestyle, I want to do it right. I also don't think I have a long conversion in me nor am I mentally and emotionally prepared. I need to know that Moira is as trusting as she seemed, and I need to know that before I fall any harder for the submissive beauty.

Dorothy and I discussed a plan.

Now, it's in motion and I'm a nervous wreck.

That longwinded explanation is why I showed up to this appointment.

"Luke, tell me why you wanted to see me today," Dr. Kizer begins as we both sit and place our mugs of coffee on a coffee table before us, me on the sofa and her in a chair with her notepad.

I think about lifting the coffee to give me something to do, but instead I turn and face Dr. Kizer. "I did it."

"You did *it*?"

The grin I've been fighting since Saturday night comes to my face.

From my perspective as a Dominant, I think one of Dr. Kizer's greatest gifts is her ability to encourage people to talk and share without specifically instructing them to do so. That wouldn't work with me and while I see her manipulation, I also know how helpful she was with Beth's and my marriage.

"I went to *Lace and Leather*."

"Oh, you did." She sounds genuinely pleased. "And was it as you remembered?"

"It hasn't changed much, if that's what you're asking."

"Yet it's different?"

I sigh. "Beth's not there."

Dr. Kizer nods.

Beth isn't a lot of places.

I stand and pace the length of the doctor's office to the windows overlooking a parking lot. Staring out the windows, I say, "I didn't know if I could go inside. The whole drive I considered turning around and going home." I spin toward her. "One hell of a Dom, right?"

"Do you think missing your wife makes you less of a Dominant?"

"I don't fucking know. I thought it did. I thought the ability and desire was gone. Until I saw..." I shake my head. Was seeing Marji at the supermarket what triggered my needs or was it her mention of Dr. Kizer? "Anyway, until I called you. Prior to that, I had pushed that part of myself away."

She nods. "But you called me and we spoke about..."

Her words trail away, allowing me to fill in the blanks of our last discussion. "I did and I went to *Lace and Leather*. The staff is mostly the same. I was greeted as if years hadn't passed."

"And how did that make you feel?"

"Like riding a bike or whatever trite saying might apply. The building, the rich wood decor, the architecture, the scents...it was all as I remembered."

"That's a great start, Luke." Her head tips. "Did you want that to be a start or were you perhaps looking for the swan song?"

Taking a deep breath, I turn back to the windows. "You know, driving over there, I thought about that. I thought I'd go to the club and realize it wasn't for me anymore, not without Beth, and I'd leave more focused than ever on life with Callie."

"Is that what happened?"

"I wasn't looking. I fucking wasn't." I swallow as the guilt I've been holding in for nearly a week bubbles to the surface. "I don't want to replace..." My voice fades as my chin drops.

Dr. Kizer's voice is no longer coming from the chair. She's behind me and her tone is soft. "Luke, Beth loved you. You loved her. You still do and always will. I saw the two of you together. I saw her passion in all things. She loved life. It's not fair that she's no longer here. It's not. There's no denying that you and she have been cheated. That said, I can't imagine that your giving up what is a part of you would be what she'd want."

I suck in a deep breath. "There was this one woman. I told her I would request her again. And then I've spent days telling myself not to."

"It doesn't have to be her. Physical attraction is often conjured in the circumstances more than the individual."

Moira's blue eyes, sexy curves, yellow curls, and long blonde hair come to my mind. Her sweet, trusting voice and her demure blush make my cheeks rise. I turn to Dr. Kizer and shake my head. "Doctor, there were multiple women at *Lace and Leather*, just as there always are. The bourbon bar had many willing to take mine—or someone else's—mind off life, with all colors of masks. If it were the circumstances, any one of those women would have done."

"You're saying this woman is...special?"

"I don't know what I'm saying. All I know is that I made arrangements to meet her again."

"At *Lace and Leather*?"

"Yes. I know it's fast, but I have a plan. I want to be sure she knows what she's doing. Since last Saturday, though I've been trying my damnedest to suppress them, the feelings and desires are back. Fuck, they're right here and I need to know if she can handle them."

"Is she experienced?"

I shake my head. "White mask."

Dr. Kizer inhales in an uncharacteristic show of emotion.

"I know. I know," I say. "Hell, I know the right way to do this. I've done it, before Beth and with Beth."

"Tell me something, Luke."

"What, Doctor?"

"This plan of yours, is it to reassure yourself that she's ready or are you trying to scare her away? What if this life is for her, but not with you? Is that fair to her?"

Fuck. I hadn't thought of it like that.

My neck straightens.

That isn't totally accurate; I have thought that maybe Moira is meant for someone else. Could I really be lucky enough to meet two women meant for me?

The truth is that if Moira isn't the woman for me, I sure as hell don't want her with some other Dom, one who could do her harm. Bringing a novice into the BDSM lifestyle takes the right Dominant.

"Luke?"

"I don't want her with someone who could...you know how some people are. Not all women are like Dorothy."

"What if this woman is?"

"Then she will be able to handle what I have planned."

I look down at my watch. It's 10:45.

"Do you want to talk about your plan?" she asks.

"I don't. I guess I wanted someone to know, someone besides Dorothy, that I want to try."

"I hope that's true, for your sake and this woman's."

"Doctor, I'll call and make another appointment. I have a meeting at eleven thirty, and I need to go." I reach for the doorknob to leave.

"Luke?"

I stop.

"You have my phone number if you need to talk."

"Thank you, Dr. Kizer."

As I pull the office door open, I take in the empty front office and sigh. Seeing Marji will need to wait for my next appointment.

If there is a next time.

*T*he words on my screen fade as I shake my head. Dr. Kizer is probably ready to fire me. Since last Saturday I've been a mess. My mind is anywhere but on what I'm doing or what she's saying. As it is today, I was late and I'm over a day behind in transcribing her sessions. Before the text from Dorothy, I was having difficulty finding my usual joy with the clients' revelations. The joy they share at their discoveries is what I had wanted.

Or so I thought.

Now that I've had it, a taste of what I've only imagined, I want more than the one-time experience. I want what comes after, whatever that may be.

Now that the text arrived and I again have hope for more—though I don't know what—I can't concentrate. My mind is filled with possibilities that make my body both excited and nervous. Mr. Santana stars in all my thoughts and dreams. He's larger than life and yet such a mystery.

Before I left the club, Dorothy mentioned that he was at one time sought after.

I keep replaying our conversation in my head.

What did she mean by at one time?

Why isn't he now?

She also said there's no rule for monogamy.

Could he be married?

I don't want to think about that possibility. As my mind wanders I recall a few clients who weren't responsive to Dr. Kizer's recommendations. Truly they're few and far between, but it happens when one partner is more open than the other.

What if he's at *Lace and Leather* to fulfill desires that his wife won't?

I'm not looking for forever, but I'm also not looking to ruin someone else's forever.

I wish I could say I looked at his hand. I wish I could say I confirmed his marital status.

I can't say either one.

The whole experience from the moment he turned on the light in the room near the back of my viewing room was overwhelming. And once he entered, I was...I am not certain how to describe it even to myself.

What happened was an out-of-body experience with all the perks of an in-body encounter. Just the memory of the way my body responded to his deep and controlling timbre causes my flesh to heat while simultaneously prickling it with goose bumps.

"Good night, Marji."

Dr. Kizer's voice pulls me from my licentious thoughts. I clear my throat. "Good night, Doctor."

Before reaching the door, Dr. Kizer stops and turns my way. "Marji, is everything all right?"

I sit taller. "I'm sorry I was late this morning. I overslept, but it won't happen—"

"No," she says waving her hand. "That's not it. I don't know what it is. You seem..." She tilted her head. "Did something happen?" When I don't respond, she goes on. "Please remember I'm here if you want to talk."

My lower lip disappears behind my teeth for a moment. No wonder she's so successful. She opens the door for confessions. Smiling, I shrug. "I-I met a man."

A smile spreads across her face, showing not only in her white teeth but also radiating from her eyes. "Then I was right, something did happen."

"I met him and I can't stop thinking about him."

"Well, in my experience that's a good thing."

"I'm nervous."

"Why?"

I shrug again. "I don't know."

"Have you gone out on a date?"

A date?

If she means have we been intimate, yes. If she means have we gone out for dinner and drinks, no. My cheeks heat as I recall the way Mr. Santana sucked my essence from his fingers—hardly an ordinary first encounter.

"We met at a club, but we are going to see one another again this weekend."

"Remember what you said before," she asks, "about not being part of a couple?"

"I'm still not."

"Maybe not, but you're a step closer. Did you ask to see him again?"

My nose wrinkles. "No."

"A strong, independent woman like you shouldn't shy away from making the first move."

"That isn't what your notes tell me."

Dr. Kizer laughs. "My advice is to explore desires, convey them to someone you trust, and when that someone trusts you in return, rejoice in your discoveries."

"It was just once," I confess.

"So he asked you out again?"

Sort of.

I nod.

"I also don't advise on gender-specific roles in a relationship. That's up to the couple."

"But all your clients seem gender..." I'm unsure how to finish the sentence.

"Currently, but I've also had client couples where the female partner is dominant and the male partner is happy to be submissive. Intimate play doesn't always mirror real life either. In everyday life the two individuals can be completely equal partners or hold the opposite roles.

There are no rules. Sometimes a couple wants a break from the reality of everyday. Role playing can provide that outlet."

I don't care if that is what others want. I know after one taste, it isn't what I want. A smile comes to my lips. "You know there are people who like vanilla ice cream, too."

She grins. "Is that you?"

"No, I'm beginning to think vanilla isn't my favorite. I'm not judging others for their choices or what they desire, but I believe I'm attracted to this man for tendencies that I didn't perceive as submissive. Quite the contrary."

"Then maybe it's better that you let him ask you for the second date."

"I guess I won't know until I go."

"Good night, Marji. That man is lucky to have met you."

"Good night."

As the door closes, I wonder if what she said is right. I've never been a big believer in luck, but that doesn't mean it doesn't happen. Maybe I'm the lucky one. The only thing I know for certain is that no matter what happens, meeting Mr. Santana is unforgettable.

A few minutes later, I give up on the transcription and check Dr. Kizer's schedule for tomorrow. She's booked solid from nine in the morning until four in the afternoon. There isn't even a break for lunch. I make a mental note to remember to bring in something to eat.

Thankfully, Fridays begin and end earlier than the rest of the week. The clock on the corner of my screen reads 7:15. While I know I should stay and try to catch up, all I can think about is what's waiting for me at home. If I don't leave now, I won't get it until tomorrow.

I recall the text I sent back to Dorothy, explaining that I would be at work all day and it would be better to have Mr. Santana's delivery go to the community leasing office. At least I know the package arrived. I received the text message from the leasing manager letting me know I can pick it up before the office closes at 8 p.m.

I thought about having the package delivered to Dr. Kizer's office, but I was afraid if I did, the doctor might ask about it or even that maybe Mr. Santana could be or had once been a client.

If that were the case, he would recognize the address.

As it is, Dr. Kizer asked what was going on with me. Having a package would have raised more questions.

Driving to my apartment, horns honk as I slam on the brakes avoiding a near-miss collision with the car in front of me, the one that came to a sudden stop. My vision flashes to my rearview mirror, thankful that the driver behind me is paying better attention than I.

Damn, my mind is everywhere but on what I'm doing.

The clock on my dashboard tells me that I have less than ten minutes to get to the leasing office. If the traffic doesn't start to move, I won't be able to pick up his package until tomorrow.

What could it be?

I've reread Dorothy's text multiple times.

YOUR PRESENCE IS REQUESTED AT LACE AND LEATHER THIS FRIDAY NIGHT AT 8 P.M. MR. SANTANA WOULD LIKE TO SEND A MESSENGER WITH YOUR ATTIRE AND INSTRUCTIONS FOR THE EVENING. IF YOU AGREE TO MEET HIM ON HIS TERMS, PLEASE RESPOND WITH YOUR ADDRESS.

My attire and instructions.

His terms.

"No, Dr. Kizer," I say aloud to my empty car. "I'm confident that the man I met isn't harboring submissive tendencies. That would be me, your strong, independent assistant." It is true, yet I'm not willing to admit that aloud to my employer. Even discussing it with Dorothy was uncomfortable. I suppose in a way Dr. Kizer and Dorothy have similar roles, helping others discover their hidden desires.

I remember the couple I was watching.

Had the man in the room next door sent attire? Had he sent a red bra and red panties that the woman forgot to wear?

I tug on my lower lip as a warming tightness blooms within my chest.

What if I don't want to wear what Mr. Santana sends? What will he do?

The thoughts conjure images of the woman's skin, red and raised by the man's belt.

And then the impossible occurs to me.

What if she did it on purpose?

The tightening in my chest lowers, twisting my core as I fidget in the seat and weave through traffic.

Why is it that when I'm in a hurry, I hit every red stoplight?

The clock on my dash says 7:57 as I pull up to the leasing office.

My heart sinks at the sight of the dark windows.

Parking my car, I hurry to the door and reach for the knob.

"Sorry, we're closed."

I turn to see the man speaking. He's standing by a dark blue car.

"Do you work in there?"

"Yes. We'll open again at nine."

I exhale. "Please, I have a package that was delivered, and I will be at work tomorrow at nine. I was looking forward to getting it." I feel my cheeks heat. "It's a surprise."

The man shakes his head. "Lady, my wife is going to be upset."

"It won't take but a minute."

"Fine."

A few minutes later, I am back in my car. In the backseat is a long white dress box with a large red ribbon.

Attached to the ribbon is an envelope with my name, my real name.

My hands are shaking as I drive to my apartment near the back of the complex. Of course I had to tell Dorothy my name. I couldn't very well accept a package to Moira. We may look alike, but the ID I was required to show has my name on it, not my sister's.

I steal a glance at the long box and the envelope.

Did she tell him my name?

Once I park, I can't take the suspense any longer. Turning off the car, I hit the overhead light and reach back for the envelope, ripping it from the giant ribbon.

My hands tremble as I fight with the flap. Inside are a smaller envelope and a separate note. I read the note first.

Moira dear, your identity is safe with me. Mr. Santana brought your gift to Lace and Leather *and I arranged the delivery.*

I let out a long sigh.

Contact me if you change your mind after opening your gift. Assuming you plan to come to Lace and Leather, *please enter code 5566 when you arrive. I will meet you at the entry to the club.*

Dorothy.

. . .

I lift the smaller envelope. It's different—heavier paper, thick and luxurious in my grasp. In flowing script on the outside is *Moira*.

Nibbling on my lip, I reach for the flap while considering the out Dorothy has given me.

Is she expecting me to change my mind?

What is inside?

My stomach twists as I tug the note free.

LUCAS

"You're dressed formal again, Luke," my mother says as Callie hurries past her on her search for my father.

"Bye, Callie girl," I call.

"Bye, Dad," she says, spinning as she runs, her long golden braid swinging seconds before she disappears through the house with her suitcase in tow, calling for her grandfather.

Shaking my head, I turn back to my mother. While I don't give my parents' appearances that much thought, I'm aware that my mom is an attractive woman in her early sixties who has always had unbounded energy. Tonight she's dressed in shorts and a top with sneakers on her feet, ready for their getaway. "She loves spending time with you too," I say. "Are you sure you want to go to the cottage tonight? I can pick her up in the morning and then you and Dad can have alone time."

"Oh, nonsense, we're alone plenty. You know we love to have Callie, and she enjoys the lake. Your father has all sorts of things planned. We'll be back on Sunday. Just be prepared for her to be tired."

I recall my childhood at the same cottage at a nearby lake, swimming, fishing, and catching frogs and lightning bugs. It makes me happy that Callie is having the same experiences.

My mother's eyebrows lift. "You seem content. You know, this is two weekends in a row that you've asked us to watch her." She gazes at my attire, the dark gray suit, blue tie, white shirt, and black leather loafers.

Tonight my tie is meant to match the mask I sent to Moira.

"Are you going to tell me that you have another dinner meeting with a client?" she asks with the edge of suspicion to her tone.

I wasn't planning on saying anything. 'Hey, Mom, can you watch my daughter while I go to a BDSM club' doesn't roll off the tongue. I grin. "Thanks again for watching Callie."

My mother reaches out and wraps her fingers around my arm. "Luke, your dad and I want you to be happy. I'm not pushing you to do anything you're not ready to do, but you know Beth would want you to be happy too."

She would want you to live. Dr. Kizer's words come back to me.

"If she were here and you weren't, wouldn't you want that for her?"

While it's impossible to think of Beth with another man, my mom is right and so is Dr. Kizer.

"I know she'd want me happy." It's all I can say.

"We adored Beth and will love her forever. That doesn't mean that we can't love another woman who makes you happy."

Her sentiments are well timed. I've spent most of last night and today anticipating a call or text from Dorothy telling me that Moira changed her mind, while at the same time hoping she wouldn't.

"I do have a meeting, Mom. And it's dinnertime."

"And you are meeting..." She leaves the sentence open-ended, but I'm not willing to fill in blanks this soon.

"I'll be by Sunday evening."

"That's a whole weekend to yourself. Or maybe not to yourself?" she says as she fishes for more.

I shake my head again. "Thanks. Who knows, maybe I'll decide to head to the cottage in the morning? I could use a few hours out on a quiet lake."

"Or maybe you'll have another meeting?"

I lean in and give her a quick kiss on her cheek. "Tell Dad to back down on the snacks. Callie told me about the cookies last time."

"If you think I can tell your father what to do, you've not been paying attention."

"See you Sunday...or sooner," I say as I open the door and step outside.

"Luke."

I turn back.

"Have a *very* good meeting."

Thirty minutes later, I'm pulling past the large gates outside *Lace and Leather*, still preparing myself for a last-second cancellation. I tell myself that if that happens, I'll simply have a drink in the bourbon bar and go home.

Of course, that isn't *all* I've been telling myself. I've also been thinking about my mother's offer for the entire weekend. How is it that I can be mentally ending whatever this is between me and Moira while simultaneously making plans for the future?

Not a forever future.

Future with the simple definition of time following present.

After securing my mask, I hand my keys to the valet, Marcus, and I look up at the large renovated mansion before me. As an architect I admire the craftsmanship. As a patron of *Lace and Leather*, I feel the power within the structure as if the wood trim and dark painted walls radiate the mood. It's empowering in a way that I can't describe. Turning, I take one more long look toward the driveway as I inhale the warm summer air.

For the first time since my life stopped, I feel the anticipation of an encounter. Last Saturday's meeting was unexpected and unforgettable. Tonight will be different.

Tonight is planned.

Tonight those blue eyes will peer up at me from behind the blue satin mask and I'll be ready for what is to come.

"Mr. Santana?" Marcus says with the intonation of a question as he pulls me from my thoughts.

"Yes."

"I believe Dorothy is waiting for you in the bourbon bar. I was also told to expect your guest in another half hour."

My chest inflates as I fill my lungs.

That means Moira hasn't canceled.

"Yes," I say, "and she is to be escorted by Dorothy to the third floor. No stops in between."

"Yes, Sir. We're prepared, and..."

When Marcus's sentence doesn't end, I lift my brows.

"Sir, I wanted to say that it's good to have you back."

With one more glance at the imposing large structure, I nod. "It's good to be back, Marcus. Take care of my girl when she arrives."

His dark eyes open wider beneath his mask as I realize what I'd just said.

My girl.

Where did that come from?

"Yes, Sir," he replies, saving me from backtracking or elaborating.

As I climb the large steps, I allow what I said—my girl—to register. I don't even know Moira, not really. I know that her blue eyes are intoxicating. I know that her innocence with this way of life is like a drug to me. I had a small amount of it last week and since then my body has been crying out for more. I realize that it is patronizing and possibly misogynistic of me to consider her mine, but nevertheless, she agreed to return here to me. She may not be mine in the full extent of the word, but last week I marked her and this week I plan to do more.

The lingerie I sent for her to wear is white and blue and scandalously scant. The bustier-corset is cupless; her perfect breasts will be barely covered with an edging of lace. The bottom hem is designed to stop at her waist. The barely present panties have a sheer triangle to cover her golden curls. Her entire shapely ass will be exposed, ready for its first bite of a crop.

My hand goes to my belt buckle as my mind imagines the leather strap contacting her flawless skin. Garters attach from the front of the bustier to thigh-high stockings. And I instructed her to wear the tall black high-heeled shoes from last week, as well as how to wear her hair. The light-blue satin mask is the final piece.

Moira can't possibly know what colors represent, but Dorothy does.

When she saw the mask, she looked up at me in question.

Thursday morning:

"Mr. Santana, accepting the status of being paired should be a decision made by two."

"Moira accepted my invitation. In time she'll understand the meaning of the color. In the meantime, I have no intentions of other men assuming her status as anything that would encourage or even garner their attention."

"Moira is a beautiful woman. I'm most certain she'll earn attention, especially in this." She pointed to the contents of the box.

"Look further."

Dorothy peeled back the lower tissue paper to reveal a long white cape trimmed in blue to match the lingerie as well as the mask. She grinned. "It seems you thought of everything."

"I want to know that she is confident in herself. As you know, this lifestyle requires strength on both sides. I'm not interested in a sub who is looking for something I don't want to provide."

I enjoy providing the control and domination. Inflicting pain for the purpose of pleasure is my wheelhouse. I also want a woman who enjoys submitting without losing her identity, a woman who can separate personal from life, a woman who is confident in her skin every day as well as in the bedroom or club.

Demeaning a submissive isn't my modus operandi. There were no golden showers in my past nor will there be in my future. That doesn't mean I won't provide punishment when warranted. However, I prefer a sensual woman laid out for my pleasure, taking the sting of a belt or crop and enduring the bite of clamps until her mind and body are entirely focused on me. It's then that I can take both of us to untold heights.

"Mr. Santana," Dorothy said, "there's a reason you're

good at what you do. You have a knack for sensing what a woman wants. Too bad really. Perhaps if I'd been wearing a white mask when we met..."

A grin came to my lips as I lifted my hand to her red hair. "Beautiful Dorothy, I don't believe even a blue and white pinafore and ruby-red slippers would disguise your incredible strength. Your stamina is legendary."

Her head tilted. "As is yours, Sir. I'd be willing to give it a go. Can you imagine the pair we'd be?"

"My dear, topping from the bottom is endearing on you."

"You can't blame a girl for trying." Her smile attempted to be demure. "You could punish her."

I refocused our conversation. "Thank you for delivering this to Moira. Please contact me immediately if you hear from her or she changes her mind after receiving the delivery. If she doesn't cancel, I want room four on the third floor."

"Room four?" she said, her eyes opened wide.

"Has it changed?"

"No, Sir. It's as you recall."

"Bring her to room four."

"As you say."

Present:

Jonathon opens the door to the club. "Mr. Santana."

"Jonathon, isn't it about time you took a night off?"

"No, Sir. Not on a weekend. I couldn't live with myself if anything ever went wrong."

While the club has a strict admission policy, BDSM and abuse are separated by a very thin line. Jonathon's chosen role is as protector and moderator. He's a true Dominant at heart who sees the safety of all submissives as his purpose.

"You're a good man."

Jonathon nods as I step through the next set of doors and make my way to the bourbon bar. When I enter, I find Dorothy standing near the shiny long bar, talking to a man in a dark suit with a black mask. Though I hate to interrupt, the clock is ticking closer to eight, to Moira's arrival.

"Would you like a drink?" the bartender asks. She's a different woman than from the other night. This one has light brown hair and is wearing a leather bustier. Her mask is adorned with rubies.

"No, thank you," I say.

At the sound of my voice, Dorothy turns, her usual mask replaced by one of silver satin indicating that she's available and interested in a softer experience. A smile spreads across my face. "Dorothy, you're full of surprises. Where's the pinafore?"

Taking a step away from the bar, she grins. "I thought maybe you wouldn't be as afraid of me if I passed on the rubies for one night."

"Oh, but I am afraid of you," I say with a grin.

She shrugs. "Topping from the bottom."

"Have you considered topping from the top?" I ask.

Her eyes open wide. "I have considered..."

"I know this great club. It's called *Lace and Leather*. You should give it a try. Perhaps there's a man...or a woman...who would indulge your fantasy."

She loops her arm through mine. "It's my fault really," she says as we begin to leave the bar.

"What is?"

"When I saw that woman, I thought of you. And then you appeared as if it was meant to be. I should have kept you for myself when I had the chance."

Instead of answering directly, as we ascend the stairway, I ask, "Moira didn't contact you again? She didn't cancel or call with questions?"

"No, Sir."

A buzzing sound comes from her side. Dorothy reaches into the pocket on her skirt and removes what looks like a beeper. Her eyes meet mine.

"Sir, if you can take yourself the rest of the way up, your partner has just passed the gate."

"I can find my way. Bring my girl to me."

Dorothy nods.

Straightening my shoulders, I continue upward, well aware of what I'd just said, how I'd claimed Moira as my own. My sense of satisfaction grows, pleased with myself for using the qualifier.

My girl.

"Come on up, Moira," I say to myself. "I'm ready to make you mine, if only for the night."

*M*y palms slide over the steering wheel and my heart beats wildly, sending my circulation racing as I fight to move forward and pull my car up to *Lace and Leather*.

The saying nervous wreck comes to mind. That's exactly what I am.

Last week I had no idea what I would find at *Lace and Leather* and yet, tonight with many ideas racing through my mind, I'm even more nervous.

I look down at my lap; the lingerie Mr. Santana sent is hidden below the thick satin cape. My hands are extended through openings on each side trying to maintain their grasp of the wheel as my high-heeled shoe presses on the brake. The cape covers me completely to mid-calf, yet it doesn't latch except for one button near the neck.

Once the shock of the attire settled, I worried about

the twenty-five-minute drive from my apartment to the club. It would be my luck that I'd have a flat tire or a fender bender. On my way home from work today, I filled my gas tank even though it was at three quarters of a tank. I wasn't taking any chances.

Work was a blur, but at least I'm making progress on Dr. Kizer's notes. I'm caught up through Wednesday. However, each session I transcribed reminded me of why I wanted to come to this club and helped me to replace my stretched nerves with desire.

That was until I got home and prepared for tonight.

I showered and shaved, washed my hair, styled it high upon my head, covered my body with lotion, and applied makeup. I've never worn lingerie like this before nor have I worn a bustier, much less one that didn't actually cover my breasts.

Once I was fully dressed, I couldn't believe that I was the woman in the mirror. I stood there for uncounted minutes, taking in the lace, the tightening of the corset, and the sensuality of the garter belts and thigh-high stockings.

When I turned, my backside was fully exposed.

My mind went to the man with the belt.

Mr. Santana told me to wear this. He also told me not to touch myself.

The longer I stared, the more I wanted to disobey. It was a true war within my thoughts as I imagined his reaction, perhaps his punishment.

Was that what I wanted?

Without thought, my eyes closed and I teased the edge of the small triangle covering my core. It was as I brushed my clit that I realized my mistake. I didn't do more. I didn't rub or find pleasure. It was a touch, an unconscious touch as my consciousness thought about Mr. Santana. In all reality it was his fault. My entire body buzzed with anticipation.

Peering in the rearview mirror, I secure the light-blue mask over my eyes and bring the car to a stop. Immediately, the valet is at the driver's-side door. With a deep breath, I hit the button to unlock the door and wait as the door swings open. As it does, a warm summer evening breeze fills the car, catching the cape and exposing my thighs.

Instead of panicking, I simply reach for the tall gentleman's hand.

"Miss Moira, welcome."

My lips curl upward at the use of my sister's name. She really would be angry if she only knew. "Hello."

"Welcome back to *Lace and Leather*. Miss Dorothy is waiting for you inside."

"Thank you."

With my hand in his, he leads me up the stairs, either unaware of what I am wearing under the cape—even the fact that I'm wearing a cape on a warm summer night—or as unfazed by it as he is the wearing of a mask. Once we reach the entrance, he releases my hand and opens the door. Standing inside, as she had been the other night, is Dorothy. Her ruby mask is replaced with one of silver.

Her smile beams larger than life. "Welcome back, Moira."

I nod as my heart rate races and my knees tremble beneath the satin. "Thank you."

"You're lovely, dear. Mr. Santana will be pleased."

Hearing her speak his name brings warmth to my cheeks. As we begin ascending the grand staircase, I say, "Dorothy, I don't know what to do."

She reaches for my arm and leans closer. "Do whatever he tells you to do."

With each step my nerves increase. When we don't stop on the second floor, I ask another question. "What's on the third floor?"

"More secluded private rooms. Mr. Santana made a request. And just so you know, the rooms are not viewable. They're also soundproof."

My feet stutter. "Soundproof?"

"Yes. When we enter, I'll show you a call button. Since no one can hear the participants if they scream, the button is to alert us if you are no longer comfortable and want to leave or need assistance."

I'm no longer climbing the stairs. My high heels are rooted to the plush carpet covering the stained wood. "Scream." I suppose it didn't come out as a question, but in reality, the one word I repeated is filled with more questions than I can articulate.

"The other night you viewed a couple."

I nod. "She didn't scream."

"She's well-trained."

Mr. Santana's deep voice replayed in my head from last Saturday. *You have a voice. Use it. I want to hear you. I want to hear your answers. If the time comes, I want to hear your pleas and your cries of ecstasy and pain. Speak.*

I swallow. "Well-trained? That's not me."

"Dear, you can turn around right now." She shakes her head. "It would be understandable."

The length of the cape settles against my sheer-stocking-covered legs.

Do I want to turn around?

Am I scared?

Am I also excited?

"You know him...Mr. Santana," I say tentatively. "Will he hurt me?"

"You do know where you are?"

"I do. I mean...does it hurt?"

Dorothy purses her lips and shakes her head. The movements aren't a negative response to my question. If I am to guess, it's more of a disbelief in my naïveté.

"If you're not looking to receive, perhaps you should cancel and explore the idea of being the Dominant. There truly are endless possibilities."

I shake my head. No, I know what turns me on, what makes me excited. I'm nervous, but I won't turn around, not when I'm this close. Besides, for some unknown reason, I trust Mr. Santana. I straighten my shoulders. "I'm going up."

"Very well. I'll show you the call button or one last chance, I'll take you back to the door. It's your choice, Moira."

I inhale. As I do, the corset reminds me of all I've done to get this far, and I know that I don't want to turn around. "The call button."

"Very well."

We climb the second set of stairs in silence as my mind fills with stories, some I've transcribed and others I've read. I imagine the woman's red skin and her tears from last Saturday night. It's as we reach the final step that I recognize what I only let skirt my thoughts: not only am I frightened, I'm incredibly turned on. My nipples are hard as diamonds behind the lace of the corset and the satin of the cape. My core is twisted and my thighs are slick. There is no way I'll be able to hide this once I'm alone with Mr. Santana.

"Dorothy, is there a restroom?"

"If you are thinking that you should hide your arousal, may I suggest you dismiss the thought."

My neck straightens. "H-how did you know?"

"Follow me to room four. Mr. Santana reserved it for tonight."

"Are the rooms different?" I ask as we pass other doors, each well-spaced apart, indicating the rooms hidden behind the walls are large.

Dorothy smiles. "Yes."

When we stop, she knocks once. The deep voice

coming from within reverberates directly to my needy core.

"Enter."

Dorothy opens the door. Within the large room, the lighting is low. After one step, my feet again stop as I gasp, taking it all in.

"Leave us, Dorothy." His baritone timbre echoes through the large space, yet I can't see him. He's in the shadows at the far end of the room.

I turn a small circle as Dorothy speaks, saying something about the call button. Though I hear her, her words don't compute. I'm too busy taking in my new surroundings.

In the center of the room is a large circular red rug showcased from a light above.

"Remove the cape and kneel in the center of the circle."

LUCAS

I've heard it said that nothing can compare to what one conjures in the imagination.

Watching Moira, I couldn't disagree more.

The memories I replayed in my head as I took care of business under a cool spray of my shower didn't come remotely close to the reality of her here with me.

This woman is stunning as she reaches for the top button of the cape, her gaze still searching the room, room four. It's one of the largest rooms in the club, fully decorated and supplied with every toy and implement relevant in BDSM play. It's a room often reserved for people like Dorothy, those wanting a more painful experience.

Most of the accessories are visible; the painted dark red walls are lined with indirect lighting, showcasing hooks and glass cases. It is like a scene from a popular movie with the wide variety of crops, whips, belts, paddles, floggers, and even canes. A large St. Andrew's cross is secured to one wall, complete with bondage apparatus. The large bed to the other side has four posts. They aren't ornate but sturdy and reinforced with metal to withstand the visible bondage cuffs. Off to the side is a spanking bench designed for multiple positions, including one that would secure the submissive's ankles as she lies back with her legs spread high in the air and her pussy exposed.

The clothing I sent was to gauge Moira's self-assuredness. This room is to test her willingness to discover her fantasies.

As she removes the cape, my breath leaves my chest. *Holy fuck.*

She was gorgeous in her black dress and without it, but tonight she is a true vision of loveliness as sexuality, sensuality, willingness, and even anxiousness seeps from her being. The emotions create a cloud of desire that makes me want to taste her, suck her, and drive her to frenzy before we even start.

Moira stills with her cape in hand.

"Drape it over the stool near the spanking bench," I say, wondering if she has any idea what most of these things are and how they are used.

"Spanking...?"

I stand, yet I know from my position and the lighting that she still can't see me. "Don't make me wait, gorgeous. I don't like to wait."

She takes a step toward the bench. "Is this...?"

"You were instructed..." My timbre has slowed. "...to enter the circle and kneel."

Without my reassurance, she finds the bench and drapes the cape over the leather surface of the smaller stool. Turning with her sexy neck straight and tall, wearing the shoes I requested, she walks into the circle of light. Bending her legs, she gracefully falls to her knees, sits back on her calves, and with her back straight, bows her head.

Good girl.

I'm getting harder by the minute.

Either she's done this before or she has researched it.

Her pert tits heave against the lace of the corset, half globes revealing the reddening tops of each areola. I think about the case filled with different clamps as my dick continues to grow. Slowly, I step from the shadows. My leather shoes tap the marble floor. As I get nearer, her face tilts upward. Though I am dying to see her blue eyes, this is about training.

"Eyes down. I haven't given you permission to look up."

Immediately her chin snaps to her chest. "I'm sorry, Sir."

"And your hands belong on your thighs, palms up, fingers and arms relaxed."

Without looking up she complies. And while it's nearly indistinguishable, I hear her humph. The sound makes my cheeks rise. I would guess that *relaxed* isn't how she's feeling at the moment. It is, however, the way I want her to feel, relaxed and trusting. That will take time.

Time?

Is that what I want?

For over two minutes I walk around her, circle after circle, taking in her tight round ass, her heady breaths, and the way her thighs press tighter together.

"In my note, I gave you a safe word. Do you remember it?"

"Yes, Sir."

I wait. Finally, I say, "I need to hear it."

Her blue eyes look my way. "Sir, I remember it. I don't want to say it. I'm only supposed to use it when I want everything to stop. I don't."

I stifle a grin.

Damn, she's adorable.

The word is cupcakes. I don't know why. It is a word not often mentioned during BDSM, one that would definitely get my attention. If she doesn't want to say it, I'm not forcing the issue. I have battles to choose and training to continue.

"Eyes down."

Resuming her position, Moira remains silent.

Walking away, I make my way to the wall with the crops and floggers. Over the last few days, I've imagined baptizing her with fire, using a cane or a thick leather strap. That was what I insinuated to Dr. Kizer. That was before. Now that she's here wearing what I sent, I can't do that. I don't want to.

There's something about this woman that makes me want to please and protect as much as I want to hurt.

Even measures.

The tips of my fingers graze over the different crops until I find one with a slender, semi-stiff handle covered in leather with a folded leather strap at the end. It will redden her skin with a quick bite, but won't strike hard enough to leave her sore or harm her beautiful skin. With it secured in my grasp, I make my way back to the radiant woman still kneeling.

Taking the crop, I run the leather over her slender shoulders, with just enough pressure to tease. As I do, her flesh prickles with goose bumps. When I stop in front of her, I bring the end of the crop under her chin and lift. "Look up, Moira."

I'm momentarily stilled by the serenity of her stare.

"Are you scared?" I ask, keeping emotion from my tone.

"No, Sir."

Her voice washes over me like a liquid melody. I feel its life-giving tune as well as hear it. And then I consider her answer.

She isn't scared.

If this is her first time, she should be. Yet she claims not to be. "Rule number one is complete and total honesty at all times. That's not negotiable. If you lie to me, you will be punished. If it happens repeatedly, we will be done. Tell me again, are you scared?"

"No, Sir. I'm not." Her lips curl into a smile. "I was,

Sir. I almost didn't make it here, to the club or up the stairs, but now that I am...here, with you...I'm not scared."

"You don't know me."

Her gaze doesn't leave mine. "I don't, but I trust you. You may prove me wrong." She quickly looks around the room before back to me. "This may all be wrong. I may be wrong for wanting to be here, for wanting to be with you. However, the answer to your question is still no, Sir, I'm not scared." Her nipples push against the lace.

"What are you?"

"I'm excited, anxious, and..." Her cheeks fill with a flash of pink.

"Talk to me, gorgeous. I want your voice."

"What about my screams?"

"What?" I ask, taking a half step back.

MARJI

"*My* screams, Sir."

Mr. Santana extends his hand, gesturing for me to rise. "Come with me, Moira."

Come with him.

Where?

I don't ask. I take him in. His suit tonight is gray and his tie matches the color of the mask he sent for me. He's a tall man, as tall as I'd remembered. Though I can't see the entirety of his face, I see his strong chiseled chin, high cheekbones, and firm lips.

I lift my hand to his and marvel at the way it fits within his grasp. His steady support helps me stand. In just the short time I've been kneeling, my feet are prickly. Shifting my weight, I fall into him.

In one swift move, he reaches down, cradling me behind my back and under my knees, and effortlessly lifts me into his arms. The gesture is oddly reassuring as I melt against his broad chest. At the same time, his chest inflates as his nose comes close to my hair. It's as if he's taking in my scent.

It's weird and hot as his rich cologne fills my senses.

Mr. Santana lowers me to the edge of the giant bed and helps me to lie back against the soft cover. His finger comes to my lips. "Honesty works both ways, Moira. I don't know why you'd mention screams, but you did. If you're asking if I want those..." He doesn't wait for an answer. "eventually, yes. However, I would venture to guess that what I want isn't what you're thinking."

What am I thinking?

My gaze goes to the St. Andrew's cross. From where I'm lying, I can only see the top, but I know what it is, what it's used for.

There's one of those in each of Dr. Kizer's cabins. I've transcribed the notes as the Dom describes the scene. In many cases it's like a ritual for him, binding his wife, his submissive, knowing he's going to bring her pain while the submissive willingly accepts her fate. The women's accounts vary but only by perspective. They speak about the cleansing release that comes with a cane or a whip, how the world's pressures no longer matter as the only thing they can think about is the searing pain. They describe it favorably. It seems wrong, yet upon entering *Lace and Leather*, right and wrong no longer seem to apply or maybe those words take on different meanings.

"Moira, look at me."

I do, and I'm lost in his dark stare, the intensity and realness.

"Tell me what you're thinking. Tell me why you mentioned screams," he demands, yet the edge from earlier has smoothed.

"Dorothy," I answer honestly.

His brow furrows. "Dorothy? What the fuck?"

I nod. "She said this room is soundproof and people can't hear my screams." There's a micro-expression or twitch that I can't identify in Mr. Santana's lips. I go on, "She told me there's a call button to push if I want to leave." My head moves up as I try to look around. "I don't know where it is. I guess I was overwhelmed walking in here."

His knuckle caresses my cheek. "Moira, do you want to be here, with me?"

"Yes, Sir. You're all I could think about this week. I swear, I am about to lose my job."

His cheeks rise as he grins. "You've been on my mind too. The room is soundproof. That's a fact. I'll be happy to point out the call button. I won't lie to you. One day I want to hear you scream, but not from pain. A well-trained submissive doesn't scream with pain. A vocalization is voluntary. You can control it. A well-trained submissive will remain silent unless instructed otherwise."

I stare upward, hearing not only his words but the care in which he delivers them. He's talking about hurting me and me not crying out and yet I'm not afraid. He makes it sound like a goal to achieve.

When I don't verbally respond, Mr. Santana shakes his head as his gaze lowers to my breasts and below. "The way you knelt, I thought maybe last time wasn't your first experience."

"With this?" I ask, clarifying his comment. "With all of this, it was my first time. If you are asking if I'm a virgin, I'm not."

Mr. Santana chuckles. "Neither am I. I wasn't asking, but now that we have that out of the way..."

I can feel the heat in my cheeks. "I didn't think you were."

"Yet you know some things about this." His gaze moves about the room.

I don't want to mention my work. "I have read and listened to things. I guess I wanted you to think I knew what I was doing so you'd be real with me."

"Do you know what you're doing?"

My head shakes. "No, Sir, but I want to learn."

His gaze slides over my body, from my face to my high heels, each inch bringing heat to my skin as if flames are growing stronger into a raging wildfire within his dark orbs. "You're stunning in the gift I sent you."

His praise fills me with warmth.

"Scoot up the bed. I'll show you where the call button is."

Doing as he says, I move until my head is upon the pillow. "Sir?"

His dark stare meets mine.

"I'm not scared. I don't need the button, but I don't understand about the screams."

"Beautiful Moira, the time to scream isn't as I bring you pain. It's as I bring you pleasure."

Like fireworks in my circulation, his explanation heats my blood, racing it to where my core clenches.

"Tell me," he demands, with a deepening tone. "Would you be willing to learn how to hold the screams back until the pleasure arrives?"

Yes. Yes. A thousand times yes.

"Yes, Sir."

"Lift your hands. I'm going to make sure you don't change your mind about the call button."

I do as he says as soft lamb's wool-lined leather cuffs are secured around each of my wrists.

"Talk to me, gorgeous."

I'm still looking up at the cuffs. "They're bigger than I imagined."

"They're wide so they won't leave a mark." He does something over my head and the cuffs lower. "Now roll over. I want to get a better look at your beautiful round ass."

It's not easy to move with the cuffs, yet I do. Once I'm rolled over, he helps me lift to my knees and elbows. Then, he again adjusts the cords connected to the cuffs and hooks my wrists together.

After everything is in place, Mr. Santana goes back to the circle of light and retrieves the crop. The bed dips as he comes closer. Slowly, he drags the crop over the skin of my neck, shoulder, back, buttocks, and thighs. "No more talking. No screams. Only noises that you can't yet control." The crop teases my cheeks. "Tears aren't voluntary. They're involuntary. Your tears are a gift."

I swallow as the sensations around me grow stronger.

The scent of his cologne.

The way his weight moves the mattress.

The ghostly touch of the crop.

They all work together to build my anticipation, causing me to fidget upon the soft bedding.

"Spread your knees farther apart."

Awkwardly I do, knowing that the evidence of my earlier arousal is still present. I gasp as the crop slides between my legs and between my folds.

His toned chest comes close to my back as he whispers in my ear. "You're fucking amazing. The best gifts you can give me are tears and a warm, wet pussy."

Two things that I can't control.

I bite my lower lip, stopping myself from responding. With each second, he continues tracing my skin as my expectancy builds.

"Two words, Moira. You will give me two words that will decide what happens next. Remember that honesty is not negotiable."

The crop slices through the air as it lands upon my ass. My entire body trembles as the biting sting radiates beyond the site he contacted. Like the crack of a window, the sensation webs through me. I fidget upon the cover and then it happens again and again in rapid succession.

Tears teeter on my lids yet I don't want it to stop. I find myself anticipating the next strike, yet his rhythm isn't predictable. All other thoughts leave my mind as I focus solely on the crop heating my flesh and taking my breath. I fight to stay still as my core tightens, needing more, wanting more. It's erotic in a way I never imagined.

His lips are near my ear and his deep timbre rumbles over my freshly spanked skin. "Yes, Sir or no, Sir."

I take a deep breath.

"I gave you one instruction before we parted ways. I told you not to touch this pretty pink pussy."

I suck in a breath as the crop glides over my core.

"I told you what would happen if you did." The crop continues to tease as I writhe against the stimulation. "I'm not going to ask you if you remember what I said because if you don't, that would require a severer punishment. I'm going to ask you only one thing. Moira, did you obey?"

The thought of lying never enters my mind.

"No, Sir."

MARJI

a shriek fills the air following the whistle of the crop and slap. Though I know the sound escaped from the depths of my throat, echoing throughout room four, I don't recall releasing it. It wasn't my plan, yet I can't recall why. Gasping for air, I grip the soft covers beneath me as my forehead falls to the same silky surface. Tears now coat my cheeks, gliding from beneath my light-blue mask, and yet through it all, those auxiliary sensations barely register.

Rapid-succession singular strikes on my sensitive core morph like a cloud mushrooming higher and higher into the sky until it's one prolonged overwhelming conscious-ness of being. I struggle for breath, attempting to keep my future cries inaudible as the rest of the world, the room, everything except Mr. Santana's actions vanish.

It isn't a fog that slowly descends as I've heard it described.

The escape from reality is instantaneous as if a curtain has fallen.

The lights are out.

Everything else is gone.

Zapping electricity such as I could never imagine streaks through my body. Originating at my core, the impulses created by the strike of the crop to my tender skin flash, coursing with lightning speed in all directions until my flesh peppers with goose bumps, my skin glistens with the sheen of perspiration, and every hair on my body stands to attention. Like a lightning rod in a thunderstorm, I fight to maintain my position, to fulfill my purpose. The winds blow stronger, bending me, pushing me until my body collapses upon the bed.

No longer kneeling, as I'd been told, I'm floating in a turbulent sea of sensory stimulations. I hear my heart beating in my veins, my ragged breaths, and his deep baritone timbre rumbling through the mayhem.

Strong sure hands roam across my hypersensitive skin. They are no longer centered only at my core, but caressing me—all of me. Mr. Santana rolls me to my back as he continues to caress. The room is no longer echoing with my cries of pain. Instead, the noises dancing around us are comprised of moans and whimpers indicative of my wanton needs.

Are those sounds coming from me?

I can't be certain of anything until dark eyes come into view, penetrating the obliteration his punishment brought and settling me like an anchor in the center of a storm. The gleaming brown orbs stare down at me as the musk of expensive cologne fills my senses and the firmest of bodies covers me. I try to hold on, to reach for his shoulders and yet my hands are still bound above my head.

Tender words begin to register as firm lips kiss my cheeks, neck, and shoulders. Lower and lower he moves, inch by inch. Such as an explorer in the wilderness, he investigates every peak and valley, kiss by kiss, until he stops just above my core.

The dark eyes are back. The warmth of his body is again over me.

"You amaze me, Moira. You're so strong. I'm proud of you."

His tone brings his praise to life, reverberating through me and lessening the sting left behind from his crop.

"Good girls deserve a reward."

His large hand cradles my chin, drawing my gaze to his as his thumb wipes away a new tear that escaped my mask. I'm not aware that I'm crying or certain of why. I've never been this overwrought with a kaleidoscope of emotions. When my eyes flutter shut, I see the colors spinning, uncertain of what they mean.

His voice comes back, causing my lids to open.

"Or this can end...if it is too much."

End?

Confusion cools my skin.

"Moira," he says firmly, "this is how this works. You have the power to make this stop. Is that what you want?"

Exhaling, I thank the stars that his words are registering, yet my body is still too overstimulated to respond verbally. I move my head. It isn't much, a little shake from side to side. All the while my mind is yelling, even begging, for this to continue, for my promised reward.

I don't want this to stop.

Please don't stop.

I've never been more focused on my needs in my entire life.

Mr. Santana's cheeks rise. "You're saying you want your reward?"

"Y-yes, Sir." My ragged voice finds its way to my tongue as Mr. Santana lowers his face near mine, the slight bristle of his cheek connecting with my dampened one.

"You're perfect." His words rumble near my ear.

My eyes close as he moves down my body, lifting my legs, spreading my thighs. I feel the movement, yet my energy is gone. I'm a puppet for his pleasure—a rag doll —capable of only moving as he positions, pulling the strings. There's warm breath at my tender core. I don't have time to register.

"Oh!" My scream is even louder than before as his tongue breaches my folds, finding my tender punished core. Without warning, my entire body convulses, from without and within. I've never been blindsided by an orgasm before, and yet that's what is happening.

My inside clenches as my wrists fight the restraints. I'm incapable of comprehension or cognitive thought. I'm raw and primal. I'm sensations and orgasms. Time means nothing as I writhe and wiggle.

Lap after lap, nip after nip. His teeth graze my swollen clit. His tongue delves deeper. Mr. Santana doesn't slow his assault—or is this reward?—sucking and nipping as fireworks explode while simultaneously each nerve within me winds tighter.

"Please, Sir," I beg as the pleasure continues to build to a painful new pitch.

"Yes, Sir or no, Sir," he says, "I need to be inside you, now."

Pulling against the restraints, my body regains some control. "Please, Sir. Please, I've never wanted something or someone this much."

I barely register as he sits back on his haunches, unlatches his belt, unbuttons his slacks, and lowers his silky boxers. Such as I'm watching a movie, he's there with his glorious penis in view—hard and thick, the tip glistening with his need as it grows even larger.

Has delirium set in?

The scene seems too perfect to be real.

I can't believe this ideal specimen of a man is with me, taking me and fulfilling my fantasies. With a condom in place, Mr. Santana leans forward and lavishes his newfound attention upon my breasts.

"Next time, I want to punish these tits...the stripe of a crop and clamps. They'd look stunning with clamps as your nipples harden..."

Next time... those words dominate his speech.

He said next time.

I try to listen and comprehend, but I can't concentrate beyond the probe of his length against my tummy as I lift my knees higher, wanting—no, needing—him inside me.

One finger, then two, expose my entrance and sink deep inside me. I let out a sigh as they bend, teasing my nerves and bringing me higher.

"Moira, you honor me with your tears and your wet pussy." He adds a third finger. "Fuck, you're so tight."

"Please..." My lip disappears beneath my teeth as he sinks into me. I try to suppress the shout as my neck strains and back arches.

"Give them to me, Moira. Let me hear your screams of pleasure."

Pleasure.

Pain.

The boundaries have blurred.

My wrists pull against the restraints as my now-hoarse voice fills the room. Deeper and deeper he thrusts, stretching my punished core until we are fully connected.

Mr. Santana stills as his dark eyes stare down at me. "Talk to me, Moira."

My head nods.

His finger moves over my lips. "Words. Let me hear your words. Tell me if you can handle this." His head shakes. "I wasn't planning...I couldn't stop."

I don't know what I see in his gaze. My overstimulated mind doesn't comprehend, yet I bow my neck upward until my lips meet with his. "Please, Sir, don't stop. I didn't know what to plan or expect. I still don't. I want this."

The domination he's shown shifts with his movements. Like a sad melody, his rhythm decelerates and a new, slow burn sparks to life inside me. Flickering like a spark to a flame, this isn't like the other orgasms he's provided. It isn't even like the pain he gave me. In some unattainable way, it is pain he's sharing with me.

It's sensual and poignant.

I feel it in my core and my soul.

Mr. Santana takes as he gives. I lose count of the times he brings me to ecstasy. And while none are as earth-shattering as the first, and my bruised core is exhausted beyond my wildest imagination, I don't want it to end.

At some point, he releases my wrists. Multiple times he replaces the condom.

No longer face-to-face, he moves me in ways I've only heard about as he continues to take me or maybe use me. I don't know which it is, and ashamedly, I don't care.

This is more of a connection than I've experienced with anyone in my entire life.

This experience is everything I imagined and more. A peaceful bliss settles over us until, just before I fall to sleep, I realize that I don't even know his real name or he mine.

LUCAS

I hold Moira in my arms longer than I should, watching her sleep, her long eyelashes fluttering as her swollen pink lips mumble incoherent approvals—*yes, Sir...please*—and morph into a smile before going slack, her warm, soft curves curled next to my bare chest.

This wasn't my plan, not when I returned to *Lace and Leather* or ever. It's too early to think about a future with this amazing woman in my grasp, and yet that's what I'm doing. I'm not thinking about it. I'm doing anything to talk myself out of it.

I don't know her.

This goes beyond her.

It's me.

I don't deserve happiness two times in my life.

There are too many people who never find it.

Why should I find it again?

Does she want a relationship or was she just looking to fulfill a fantasy?

Did I fulfill it?

I can't be sure.

Somewhere along the way, I lost focus of my purpose to train her. I forgot that she was new. I forgot that I'd punished her or how she'd so beautifully taken each strike of the crop. All of that disappeared as my ears filled with her sounds of pleasure and her pussy strangled my dick as she came apart time after time.

It's been too long since I've found real relief, the kind that can only come within a woman. It's also been too long since I've experienced the pleasure and satisfaction that comes with sharing that, from focusing her on the present, removing the roadblocks of her mind, and centering her on her desires as well as my needs.

I hadn't planned on us going that far, and yet I'm still here—nude, long after midnight with this lovely creature in my embrace.

I've never gone this far off script with a newbie.

Maybe that's part of it—the newness.

I believed Moira when she said this way of life was new, yet she hadn't come to *Lace and Leather* blind. She'd researched—read. Her naïveté is as enticing as her knowledge is reassuring. The combination is an aphrodisiac like none I've ever known.

I can't compare her to Beth.

I won't.

And still, as I stare up at the mirror over the bed

and see this beauty with me, the one who trusts me, who gives herself willingly to me, I can only hope that my mother and Dr. Kizer are right, that Beth is happy.

If I could speak to her now, I'd want her to know that I will always love her. That will never change. I also hope she loves me enough to want me to live, whether with this woman or someone else.

Callie comes to my mind.

I have too much baggage to expect Moira to willingly be more than she is, than we are at this moment.

Taking a deep breath, I kiss her mussed hair and ease from the bed. Moira moans and with a slight shift, settles into the warm blankets. A few minutes later, I'm dressed and have a penned note in hand. Taking it to where I've laid her clothes, I lay it on top of them where she's sure to see it.

My heart races as I walk back to the bed and see that her mask is a bit askew. I wrestle with the idea of removing it and seeing the full face of the woman who, if nothing else, has brought me back to life.

Isn't that enough to ask of one person?

I have no right to ask more.

As I leave room four and quietly close the door, I straighten my shoulders and step down the silent corridor until I reach the grand staircase. It's nearly two in the morning, but I won't leave until I give strict orders for Moira to be kept alone, safe, and escorted to her car when she wakes.

I reach the first floor expecting to find Dorothy. Yet the entryway is oddly quiet.

Going to the large doors, I enter the bourbon bar.

In all the years, it has barely changed. Beneath the masks, I see a few familiar sets of eyes. It's with a sense of pride I recognize a few of the submissives as ones I'd trained.

At this hour, the bar is less formal. The cigar and bourbon aroma is replaced by the musk of sexual desire. It is as thick as fog surrounding the single patrons, couples, and small gatherings.

While the Dominants are mostly clothed in their finest, the submissives are more often stripped to an outfit similar to the one I sent for Moira—corset or bustier, stockings with garters, and high heels—or completely bare. That may be an overstatement. Those submissives, the ones without clothes, are often wearing a collar attached to their master's leash and a splash of other adornments, such as clamps like the ones I mentioned to Moira or gags forcing their mouths open in a constant state of readiness for their master's desires.

The genders occupying the different roles vary.

I think of Dorothy, wondering if she has or will give the dominant side of her a chance to explore. While she enjoys the bite of a bullwhip, I am confident she'd find equal pleasure in delivering the blows.

Near the back of the bar is a table of Doms playing what I know from experience is high-stakes poker. These players can place a ten-thousand-dollar bet while their subs kneel between their knees with their cocks in their mouths.

Currently, it appears that each player's submissive is kneeling near his or her chair. Their heads are respectively bowed as they sit back on their bent toes with their backs straight. It's a painful position to maintain for a prolonged period of time. However, if they do, they will be rightfully rewarded. If they don't, they will be justly punished.

"Mr. Santana."

I turn to the sound of Dorothy's voice. "Perhaps you'd like to join the poker game. I believe a chair will be opening soon."

We both watch as one of the submissives crawls toward her master, rubbing her forehead against his thigh. He reaches down to pet her hair, like an owner satisfying a cat. It's then she takes his fingers, sucking them deep beyond her lips as she wiggles in her stance. It's a violation of most Doms' rules, and will most likely result in her desired outcome. Whether reward or punishment is in her future, soon the two of them will be disappearing to a more private room.

"I'm leaving," I say. "First, I wanted to make it clear that Moira isn't to be disturbed until she wakes. Once she does she's been instructed to push the call button. At that time, she should be escorted to her car." I scan the bar, seeing the Doms without submissives, the ones stirring their drinks as they watch the various couples. The hair at the nape of my neck stands to attention. "She's to be in contact with no one but you."

Dorothy nods. "Any message for her, Sir?"

"I left her a note. She will relay her response to me through you."

"As you wish."

My head tilts. "You're being very agreeable tonight."

"If I weren't would you punish me?"

I shake my head. "Good night, Dorothy."

"Mr. Santana, will we see you again or is this farewell?"

I take a deep breath. "I'll be waiting for your call."

As I walk away, I feel Dorothy's stare on my back, coming from her silver mask. She's too knowledgeable at reading people. It isn't like I make it difficult. Regarding Moira, I've shown her my cards. I would be no good at that poker game. In two meetings, I've fallen hard for the woman upstairs, and now I'm putting any hope of a future into her hands.

The love I shared with Beth showed me many sides of a BDSM relationship beyond what Dorothy or others want. There's nothing wrong with a purely physical relationship—giving pain and seeking it. I did that in my earlier years. I'd trained submissives so that they could go on and find what was right for them.

That is no longer enough. I want the whole package. I want to live beyond a weekly session at *Lace and Leather*. I want a life with someone who not only wants what I want and what I need but also wants more, someone who trusts me and whom I trust, someone who can live this life and also live in the reality of everyday.

As I wait for my car to arrive, I know that to achieve my goal, the first step is to know one another's real name. That means a relationship beyond masks and anonymity. It means I should listen to my mother and Dr. Kizer and begin a real relationship outside these walls.

MARJI

The sun is rising as I settle behind my steering wheel with my cape wrapped securely around me, concealing the outfit I wore to *Lace and Leather* beyond my shoes and stockings. It isn't until I'm off the grounds that I pull my car over and succumb to the tears I've barely kept suppressed throughout my conversation with Dorothy and the valet.

Turning off the engine, I lower my window as my head bows forward and tears bubble from my chest. As the soft morning breeze blows my mussed hair, deep breaths go out, and yet I can't seem to inhale, not enough to fill my lungs. With trembling hands, I remove the crumpled note from the pocket of the cape. My tear-filled eyes make the words blurry though that doesn't matter. I will never forget the gist of what he said.

. . .

MOIRA,

YOUR FUTURE IS YOURS TO DECIDE. MY RULES ARE NONNEGOTIABLE. YOU HAVE EXPERIENCED A TASTE OF THIS LIFE AND SHOWN IT ISN'T FOR YOU. GO BACK TO YOUR SAFE AND SECURE LIFE AND KNOW IT WAS A PLEASURE TO EXPERIENCE YOUR NAÏVETÉ DURING YOUR TRAINING.

THAT PART OF YOU IS MINE FOREVER. THE REST OF YOU CAN BE GIVEN TO THE PERSON OF YOUR CHOICE. MAY I SUGGEST, NOT AT LACE AND LEATHER.

YOU WILL FIND THE CALL BUTTON BESIDE THE DOOR TO THE HALLWAY. AFTER YOU ARE DRESSED, PRESS IT AND YOU WILL BE ESCORTED AWAY.

MR. SANTANA

In other words, I used you. Go on with your life. You're not really cut out for this and oh, by the way, don't come back.

I can't comprehend what went wrong or what happened. The last thing I recall is falling asleep in Mr. Santana's embrace, both of us exhausted yet satiated beyond compare.

"No, Marji." My voice is ragged from both the sobs and last night. "It was only you who was satisfied. He was only training you. You aren't special. It was sex. It was domination. That was all. There was no connection."

After a few minutes or maybe longer, I find the strength to drive to my apartment. Once inside, I spot the box Mr. Santana's outfit came in. Quickly, I strip from the clothes and stuff them back into the box. If I had his address or even his name, I'd send them back.

My sadness changes to anger and indignation as scenes from last night replay in my head.

Screw him!

I didn't go to *Lace and Leather* to find one man.

I went to experience something I wanted to experience. I did that. I faced my insecurities and I donned a mask and entered the world of the unknown. Fuck him and his training and taking my naïveté.

"No, Mr. Santana, you didn't take anything," I say louder than I should at the now-filled box. "I gave it. Not to get anything from you or anyone else in return. You can't take that from me. I did this."

My knees crumple as I fall to the floor near the box.

When I wake, I'm cold and achy. I lift my nude body from the floor and make my way to the bathroom. The woman in the mirror is a sad reflection of who I thought I'd be after this weekend. My hair is completely trashed, makeup is ruined, eyes and lips swollen, and there are other signs not visible in my reflection.

It's within me. I feel him as I walk and stand. Not only physically but emotionally too.

The notes I transcribe discuss the sustained aftereffects that come with being the recipient of punishment or simply playful pain. They say how the lingering effects bring satisfaction and contentment, reminding the recipient of what happened and how it was consensual. Gripping the edge of the sink, I remind myself that it was consensual and I did take it. My lips tease upward as I recall his praise. Just as fast they fall.

The hot water of the shower washes over me as I vow to move forward.

By Monday morning, I am mostly convinced that I can continue to go on with life as I have known it. There were a few times on Sunday that I wasn't certain. Those were times of insecurity.

Each time I reminded myself that I didn't fail. I set out to do something—try something—and I did. Mr. Santana's perception of me is skewed by his experiences. Fine, I didn't meet up. That's his problem, not mine.

When I arrive at Dr. Kizer's office, the door to her private office is closed and the light is shining through the frosted glass. It's too early for a client and yet as I approach the door, I hear her voice. My steps still as I wrestle with possibilities. Either she's on the phone or there is a client present. Lifting my knuckles, I knock.

It takes a few seconds, but the door opens inward, just far enough for me to see my employer.

"Is everything all right?" I ask. "Do you need anything?"

"No, Marji. Everything is fine. Can you please call my

ten o'clock and let them know I may be running a bit behind?"

My neck straightens. This is not like her. Punctuality is part of Dr. Kizer's magic. In sixty minutes a week she can fix what ails you. "Are you sure?"

She turns and peers where I can't see. "Yes, I'm sure."

"Okay. I'll call them right away."

"Thank you, Marji. Please don't disturb us."

"Yes, Doctor."

LUCAS

$\mathcal{L}$eaning forward, I drop my head to my hands, my elbows supported on my outstretched knees as a knock raps on Dr. Kizer's office door. It's probably her assistant, Marji, the pretty blonde. For a moment when I hear her voice, Moira comes to mind.

With a sigh, I lean back against the chair and peer toward Dr. Kizer. I can't see who she's speaking to, but I can hear Dr. Kizer use her name, Marji.

Marji isn't Moira; she isn't who I want.

Since Saturday morning, I have been hoping to see and hear Moira at every turn. Now I'm imagining her here.

After Dr. Kizer closes the door, she turns back to me. "Luke, tell me again about what happened."

Standing, I go to the window of her office and look absently down to the parking lot. I'm not seeing the cars. I'm back in room four.

"I wanted to stay with her. I considered it more than I should have."

"Why shouldn't you have wanted that?"

I sigh. "Because I don't know her." I close my eyes and face the truth. "Because I didn't want to leave her...ever. It was too fast. It was suffocating, and it would be as much for her as for me. I knew I should give her space, and when I did she shunned me."

"After she got your note saying you wanted to see her again, to learn more about the real her, she called you?" Dr. Kizer asks.

"No, Dorothy from *Lace and Leather*, she relayed Moira's message. In a nutshell, she enjoyed a noncommittal fuck and now she knows BDSM isn't for her. She's going back to her vanilla husband." My stomach again reels at that revelation. I lift my hands in the air. "How did I not know she was married?"

Dr. Kizer tilts her head. "How could you know?"

"I asked Dorothy about the questionnaire. Dorothy said she hadn't revealed that nugget of truth."

"So tell me what you did after the call from Dorothy."

"I sulked like a fucking pussy. Tell me, Doctor, tell me again how I can bring back a part of me when I'm weak. After I got my shit together on Saturday afternoon, I drove to my parents' cottage and made some excuse about wanting fresh fish. I spent the rest of the day out on the lake by myself."

"Did you catch any?"

I turn toward her. "What?"

"Did you catch fish?"

"Yeah, but what difference does that make?"

"What did you do with them?"

"I took them back to the cottage, cleaned them, and sat with my dad as my mom and Callie battered and fried them."

"Saturday night?"

"I sat with my parents after Callie went to bed and listened to the crickets and tried to act like I hadn't just been through hell."

"Sunday?" Dr. Kizer asks.

"I don't understand your questioning." I think back. "I showed Callie how to catch minnows and we all swam. Mom made dinner. This is stupid."

"Tell me again, Luke, what did you do after you got the call?"

I sink to the sofa. "I don't understand what you're asking. I told you everything I did."

Her cheeks rise as her lips curl upward. "Luke, you called and came to me recently, why?"

"Fuck, I don't know. I guess I wanted to know if it was okay to—"

"To live," Dr. Kizer finishes my sentence. "We discussed you *living*. Life changes. Our priorities change. From what you said, you enjoyed the experience of reliving fond sexual experiences. That is part of you *living*. What you did after you received Dorothy's call is also you *living*. You went to your family. You fished, caught fish, and ate fish. You spent time with your daughter and parents. You didn't fade away. You are too strong for that. You brushed it off and lived. Remember that the next time."

"Next time?"

"Luke, it doesn't have to be at *Lace and Leather*. It doesn't have to be anywhere. Life is everywhere. It's where you least expect it. A man like you won't let this one experience define him. If you can live after the tragedy life has dealt you, you can keep living."

"I guess that I feel like I had hope for the first time in a long time."

"No, Luke. Hope isn't isolated. Sometimes it feels lost, but it's still there. You know, like the car keys you can't find? They're there, but you don't see them. You saw hope in Moira. You have hope every day. One day you'll see it again."

"I see it constantly in Callie."

"And you should. We both know that's different, but that doesn't diminish it. You don't have to search for hope, but be prepared when it surfaces."

Peering down at my watch, I see that it's almost ten in the morning, the time of Dr. Kizer's first appointment. "I should go. Thank you for seeing me this morning. I know you have other patients."

"I asked Marji to give us more time."

I shake my head. "I should go. I'll set up another appointment for, say, a month. I need some time to find those keys."

Dr. Kizer grins. "Luke, you did nothing wrong. The

way you are may not be to Moira's liking, but it is to someone else's. And as for hope, it's never wrong to want it. Just keep your eyes open."

Straightening my shoulders, I nod. "Thank you again. I better go."

As I open the door, I'm again struck by the resemblance of Marji to Moira. I only see the back of her head and her slender shoulders and soft curves.

It's my imagination.

And then she turns.

MARJI

J turn toward the sound of Dr. Kizer's door opening and my entire body freezes. I'm momentarily paralyzed as the dark, penetrating stare comes my direction, latching my gaze and rocking my reality. I can't compute as I'm decimated with the calamity of worlds colliding.

Two impossible scenes become one.

While I'm staring at the man I saw recently in the grocery store with his daughter, I know in my heart, in every fiber of my body, that he's also Mr. Santana. I may not have seen the entirety of his face, but I saw him—the rest of him. The man before me is the man who brought me pain, pleasure, and satisfaction in a way I've never known.

He's also the man who rejected me.

Those thoughts and more flash through my mind as

his steps still. My vision tunnels as Dr. Kizer steps around the fringe, coming to my desk.

"Marji, could you please schedule Lucas McAroy for an appointment a month from today?" She turns toward Lucas. "Remember, you can always call or make an appointment for sooner if you change your mind."

Lucas doesn't speak. His zeroed-in stare never leaves mine as his neck straightens and shoulders broaden. It's a look I recognize, one that in only a short time I knew to mean he was about to issue a demand. It isn't the one that accompanied praise or tenderness.

Dr. Kizer takes a step back, surveying the two people before her.

"Marji, what time are the Martins coming in?" When I don't answer, she repeats the question.

I blink as I pull my gaze from Lucas and turn to my boss. Though I answer her question, my eyes fill again with tears. After this weekend, I'm not certain how I'm capable of forming more, yet I obviously do. "I'm sorry, what?" I ask, looking at Dr. Kizer.

"The Martins? I asked you to postpone their appointment."

Swallowing my emotions, I nod. "Yes, I called. They rescheduled." I sniff away my tears. "You had an opening on Wednesday and now your schedule won't be delayed."

She turns to Lucas. "Luke, do you recall my assistant, Marji?" She turns to me, "Marji, you remember Luke."

Lucas turns away. "I'll call you directly, Doctor."

Before he leaves, I blurt out, "Why?"

Lucas turns on his heels, facing me as if Dr. Kizer isn't in the room and says, "Yes, Sir or no, Sir, you let Dorothy give me your Dear John message?" He doesn't allow me to respond before adding, "Yes, Sir or no, Sir, you went back to your husband."

My eyes widen as I stand. "No, Sir, to both." My voice is no longer submissive as my indignation returns. "Your note said you didn't want to see me again. I'm not married. I never have been."

His dark stare moves from me to Dr. Kizer.

"Lucas, Marji is telling you the truth about her never being married. I don't know about the note."

Quickly, I reach for my purse. Pulling the note, now barely readable, from its depths, I hand it to Lucas. "Here, Sir. This is what I found when I woke."

Taking it from my grasp, he straightens the linen paper. As his eyes scan the page, his jaw clenches tighter and tighter and the muscles along the side of his handsome face become taut. Finally, when he looks back at me, the anger from moments before is replaced by something softer. "Fuck, Moira, this isn't what I wrote." He shakes the paper. "I didn't write this."

Dr. Kizer lets out a long breath. "It seems there is an hour free on my schedule if you two would like to talk." She grins. "With or without me."

My chest heaves against my blouse. "I thought..."

Lucas extends his hand my direction. In the microsecond that follows I see him with his daughter and then again at *Lace and Leather*, reassuring, helping, and training me. Taking in his complete unmasked face, I lift my hand to his.

As his fingers close around mine, he says, "I also thought...Well, it seems as though we were both misled."

"I don't understand," I admit.

"It may seem awkward to do it here," Dr. Kizer says, "but it appears that the two of you have a few things to settle before discussing a future."

My eyes look up at the man holding my hand. "Future?"

His broad shoulder shrugs. "It was my hope."

Walking hand in hand, we follow Dr. Kizer beyond the door to her private office. My steps still as I look around. I've been within this room hundreds of times and yet with Lucas beside me it feels different.

"I'll give you both a few minutes alone," Dr. Kizer says as she steps out, closing the door.

Lucas's free hand comes to my cheek. "Marji, huh?"

I nod. "Yes, Sir." My grin grows. "Mr. McAroy."

"Luke or Lucas."

"Sir?"

His finger rubs over my lips. "It sounds perfect coming from your lips."

My head bows against his chest. "How?" I look up, my eyes again filling with tears. "Why?"

Lucas pulls my face toward his as our lips come together. It's neither rushed nor needy. The connection is right and reassuring. As the kiss ends, he says, "I believe we were sabotaged."

"By whom...Dorothy?"

He nods. "She has always been attentive of me. I think she was surprised to see me back at *Lace and Leather*. It's been a few years..."

This time I reach up to his cheek. "Lucas, I am still sorry about Beth. I will always respect and honor the love the two of you shared. I don't know what's in our future, but I hope there's a future."

"I have a daughter."

My cheeks rise in a grin. "Who loves strawberries and chocolate pudding and makes your face light up. When you're ready...if you are...I'd love to get to know her, too." I take a step back and cross my arms over my breasts. "Now, tell me about Dorothy, about what you think happened."

His smile broadens. "Look at you all bossy."

I shrug. "When I need to be. I'm rather fond of the other way around, too. Now, tell me what you think happened."

"I'd like to get to know both sides better." His head shakes. "I never suspected she'd do something like this. It seems from that note you showed me that she relayed a false message to each of us. That note you showed me isn't what I wrote. I wrote that I wanted to meet with you away from *Lace and Leather*, to get to know you better."

"You wrote that?"

"I did." His hands reach for mine. "I still want that."

As our hands intertwine, I ask, "Why would she do that?"

"I think she wanted a chance with me." He inhales as his broad chest inflates. "She's dropped hints before. I've always played them off. They were more blatant recently. Now that I think about it, she questioned me about your blue mask."

"I thought it just matched the outfit."

Lucas squeezes my hands. "No, Marji, light blue means you're taken, that no other Dom can approach you."

I don't know if something so transparently patronizing should make me smile, but it does.

"I think that's also why she warned you about the soundproof room," he says. "I believe she was trying to frighten you."

"She did," I admit. "But I trusted you more than I was scared."

We both turn to a knock on the door. It opens and Dr. Kizer peers inside. "May I join you?"

"It is your office," Lucas says.

"Is it appropriate to welcome you both to your first session of couples therapy?" Dr. Kizer asks with a grin.

As we sit together upon the sofa I smile and look up to Lucas. "Does that mean we're a couple?"

"I hope."

EPILOGUE

Lucas

Six months later

"Y ou know my parents and Callie. They adore you, Marji. I have spent time with your parents. They seem to approve of us and even of Callie. Your father gave me permission to propose, and your mother dotes over her.

"Why are you so worried about me meeting Marshall and Sis?" It's a strange name for her sister, but since I don't have a sister, I don't have an issue calling her that.

Marji stares my direction, her blue eyes wide. "Lucas, they live so far away. I never thought..."

"That she and her husband would come here for our wedding or that in a few hours we'll all be together at your parents' house?" I take a step toward my fiancée and reach for her chin as I pull her lip from behind her teeth. "Talk to me, gorgeous. You're hiding something."

Marji shifts her footing, her telltale sign that she's stalling.

With Callie in the other room, I look around our bedroom, lean forward, and whisper menacingly in her ear, deepening my tone and slowing my timbre. "Being completely honest is a nonnegotiable rule. Tell me what's happening. Have you lied to me?"

"I-I..." Her gaze skirts to my chest and back to my eyes. "I haven't *lied*."

I don't release her chin as my grin broadens. "I'm going to enjoy watching your round ass turn red after Callie is sound asleep."

Being an architect has its advantages. After I asked Marji to marry me, I made a few adjustments to a house I was drawing with a builder. It's the house where we now live. I hadn't realized the house would be for us and our growing family when I began designing it. However, after the future became clear, I added a soundproof playroom off of our bedroom. It's only accessible through our large walk-in closet and stays locked whenever it's not in use. We also have a monitoring system that assures us that Callie is safe and asleep in her bedroom and will have the same monitors installed before the baby's room is occupied.

The first time Marji joined me in room four at *Lace and Leather*, she was out of her element. Let's just say she's advanced rather quickly. The St. Andrew's cross was her idea. The spanking chair was mine. No, she's not ready for a ruby-studded mask, and I'm perfectly fine with that. In reality, we're navigating these waters together. I have the experience, but everything is new with her enthusiasm.

Dr. Kizer says it's all about trust. It doesn't matter if we've been a couple for ten years or a matter of months. Trust is something that can only be given when it's also received. Knowing now that Marji's research stemmed from Dr. Kizer's notes explains the dichotomy in her knowledge versus real-life familiarity.

And speaking of *Lace and Leather*, we sometimes visit with Marji's light-blue mask in place. In case you're wondering, no, Dorothy is no longer there. Rumor is that she's opened a new club outside of Milwaukee. Though Marji and I have no plans to visit, we wish her well.

In reality, she is the one who brought us together.

Marji sighs. "Lucas, I would gladly let you turn my skin red, but before we meet with my family, you need to know something...something that may seem weird."

"Go on."

"My sister isn't called Sis. I made that up."

My head tilts. "Why would you do that?"

Marji's cheeks glow with a rosy blush. "My sister is my twin."

I look down at her stomach. "Are you saying we're having twins? Why didn't you mention you're a twin?"

"No, we're not having twins. You were there at the doctor's office when we had an ultrasound."

"It was all just fuzz." While I hate to admit that, it was. They said we'll see more clearly next time. I thought they'd improved those things since Callie, but apparently the 3D imaging isn't standard. Fuzz is.

"I told the doctor I am a twin—an identical twin," Marji says. "She knows and said we're only having one baby."

"Marji, I'm confused. You have an identical twin and you have never mentioned that bit of information. And on top of that, her name isn't Sis?" I reach again for her cheek. "Gorgeous, if you're worried I'll be attracted to her because you look similar—"

Her head is shaking. "No, I'm not. I mean, if you are, tell me. But Marshall, her husband, has never had a problem telling us apart. That isn't what's worrying me."

"Talk to me, gorgeous, use your words."

She lets out a long sigh. "My sister's name is..." She momentarily bites her lower lip. "...Moira."

Our bedroom fills with laugher as we both collapse onto the king-sized bed. When we turn to face one another, I give her a kiss as I gather her in my arms. "Well, now, that will be awkward."

"I'm sorry. I never expected that one night would..."

"Would be unforgettable?" I ask as I pull her over me and reach for her round ass, the one that will be at my disposal tonight. "Is that what you were going to say?"

"Yes, Sir, just like every day after it...unforgettable."

The End

Did you know that Dr. Kizer has helped other characters? If you enjoyed UNFORGETTABLE, be sure to check out and download UNCONVENTIONAL and UNEXPECTED, all stand-alone novellas in the INDULGENCE series.

Download today. Learn Dr. Kizer's secret of success while exploring hidden desires!

Click on the title to download UNCONVENTIOINAL and UNEXPECTED today.

WHAT TO DO NOW

LEND IT: Did you enjoy UNFORGETTABLE? Do you have a friend who'd enjoy UNFORGETTABLE? UNFORGETTABLE may be lent one time. Sharing is caring!

RECOMMEND IT: Do you have multiple friends who'd enjoy this short, steamy story? Tell them about it! Call, text, post, tweet...your recommendation is the nicest gift you can give to an author!

REVIEW IT: Tell the world. Please go to the retailer where you purchased this book, as well as Goodreads, and write a review. Please share your thoughts about UNFORGETTABLE on:

*Amazon, UNFORGETTABLE Customer Reviews

*Barnes & Noble, UNFORGETTABLE, Customer Reviews

*iBooks, UNFORGETTABLE Customer Reviews

* BookBub, UNFORGETTABLE Customer Reviews

*Goodreads.com/Aleatha Romig

BOOKS BY NEW YORK TIMES BESTSELLING AUTHOR ALEATHA ROMIG

WEB OF DESIRE:

SPARK

Jan 14, 2020

FLAME

Feb 25,2020

ASHES

April 7, 2020

TANGLED WEB:

TWISTED

May 21, 2019

OBSESSED

July 2, 2019

BOUND

Aug 13, 2019

WEB OF SIN:

SECRETS

Oct. 30, 2018

LIES

Dec. 4, 2018

PROMISES

Jan. 8, 2019

THE INFIDELITY SERIES:

BETRAYAL

Book #1

Released October 2015

CUNNING

Book #2

Released January 2016

DECEPTION

Book #3

Released May 2016

ENTRAPMENT

Book #4

Released September 2016

FIDELITY

Book #5

Released January 2017

THE CONSEQUENCES SERIES:

CONSEQUENCES

(Book #1)

Released August 2011

TRUTH

(Book #2)

Released October 2012

CONVICTED

(Book #3)

Released October 2013

REVEALED

(Book #4)

Previously titled: Behind His Eyes Convicted: The Missing Years

Re-released June 2014

BEYOND THE CONSEQUENCES

(Book #5)

Released January 2015

RIPPLES

Released Oct 2017

CONSEQUENCES COMPANION READS:

BEHIND HIS EYES-CONSEQUENCES

Released January 2014

BEHIND HIS EYES-TRUTH

Released March 2014

STAND ALONE MAFIA THRILLER:

PRICE OF HONOR

Available Now

THE LIGHT DUET:

Published through Thomas and Mercer Amazon exclusive

INTO THE LIGHT

Released 2016

AWAY FROM THE DARK

Released 2016

TALES FROM THE DARK SIDE SERIES:

INSIDIOUS

(All books in this series are stand-alone erotic thrillers)

Released October 2014

DUPLICITY

(Completely unrelated to book #1)

Release TBA

ALEATHA'S LIGHTER ONES:

PLUS ONE

Stand-alone fun, sexy romance

Released May 2017

A SECRET ONE

Fun, sexy novella

Released April 2018

ANOTHER ONE

Stand-alone fun, sexy romance

Releasing May 2018

ONE NIGHT

Stand-alone, sexy contemporary romance

September 2017

INDULGENCE SERIES:

UNEXPECTED

Released August 27, 2018

UNCONVENTIONAL

Released individually

January 1, 2018

UNFORGETTABLE

Released October 22, 2019

ABOUT THE AUTHOR

Aleatha Romig is a New York Times, Wall Street Journal, and USA Today bestselling author who lives in Indiana, USA. She has raised three children with her high school sweetheart and husband of over thirty years. Before she became a full-time author, she worked days as a dental hygienist and spent her nights writing. Now, when she's not imagining mind-blowing twists and turns, she likes to spend her time with her family and friends. Her other pastimes include reading and creating heroes/anti-heroes who haunt your dreams!

Aleatha impresses with her versatility in writing. She released her first novel, CONSEQUENCES, in August of 2011. CONSEQUENCES, a dark romance, became a bestselling series with five novels and two companions released from 2011 through 2015. The compelling and epic story of Anthony and Claire Rawlings has graced more than half a million e-readers. Her first stand-alone smart, sexy thriller INSIDIOUS was next. Then Aleatha released the five-novel INFIDELITY series, a romantic suspense saga, that took the reading world by storm, the final book landing on three of the top bestseller lists. She ventured into traditional publishing with Thomas and Mercer. Her books INTO THE LIGHT and AWAY FROM THE DARK were published through this mystery/thriller publisher in 2016. In the spring of 2017, Aleatha again ventured into a different genre with her first fun and sexy stand-alone romantic comedy with the USA Today bestseller PLUS ONE. She continued with ONE NIGHT and ANOTHER ONE. If you like fun, sexy, novellas that make your heart pound, try her UNCONVENTIONAL and UNEXPECTED. In 2018 Aleatha returned to her dark romance roots with WEB OF SIN.

Aleatha is a "Published Author's Network" member of the Romance Writers of America and PEN America. She is represented by Kevan Lyon of Marsal Lyon Literary Agency.

facebook.com/aleatharomig

twitter.com/aleatharomig

instagram.com/aleatharomig

CPSIA information can be obtained
at www.ICGtesting.com
Printed in the USA
LVHW021534011119
636085LV00009B/394/P

9 781947 189522